Readers love
DIRK GREYSON

Lost Mate

"Do yourself a favor and pick up this book or anything that Mr. Greyson has written. You will not be sorry."

—Harlie Williams

Darkness Rising

"This book is filled with suspense, sex and amazing characters… I give five stars to this book, this series and Mr. Greyson."

—Paranormal Romance Guild

"I can guarantee that you won't be disappointed at all. This is a fascinating story that is very unique."

—MM Good Book Reviews

Playing With Fire

"I highly recommend this book. If you love a true mystery that is hard to figure out and if you love a professor bookworm type paired with a hard-nosed with-a-heart detective, then you will love this book."

—Gay Book Reviews

"*Playing With Fire* was a great read and fans of this author, as well as those trying him for the first time, are sure to enjoy the story."

—Top 2 Bottom Book Reviews

By Dirk Greyson

An Assassin's Holiday
Flight or Fight
Hell and Back
Lost Mate
Playing With Fire

DAY AND KNIGHT
Day and Knight
Sun and Shadow
Dawn and Dusk

YELLOWSTONE WOLVES
Challenge the Darkness
Darkness Threatening
Darkness Rising

Published by Dreamspinner Press
www.dreamspinnerpress.com

DIRK
GREYSON

HELL ᴬᴺᴰ BACK

REAMSPINNER
PRESS

Published by

DREAMSPINNER PRESS

5032 Capital Circle SW, Suite 2, PMB# 279, Tallahassee, FL 32305-7886 USA
www.dreamspinnerpress.com

Hell and Back
© 2017 Dirk Greyson.

Cover Art
© 2017 L.C. Chase.
http://www.lcchase.com
Cover content is for illustrative purposes only and any person depicted on the cover is a model.

ISBN: 978-1-63533-905-5
Digital ISBN: 978-1-63533-906-2
Library of Congress Control Number: 2017905520
Published October 2017
v. 1.0

Printed in the United States of America
∞
This paper meets the requirements of
ANSI/NISO Z39.48-1992 (Permanence of Paper).

To Dominic, Elizabeth, and Lynn, because they understand that sometimes I need to kill people (in fiction, of course).

CHAPTER 1

"VINCE, I don't know what the hell to do anymore." Forge Reynolds sat in one of the client chairs in his lawyer's office, as he had so many time over the last eight months, wondering just how much more of this he could take. "I'm not asking for anything that isn't reasonable or that I'm not entitled to." He huffed slowly. This was a war of attrition, and Forge was starting to feel like a casualty.

"That's very true, but Granger has obviously decided to fight you on every point, no matter how small." Vince shook his regal head of impressively black hair. He was an unusual attorney in that he wasn't all buttoned-up and proper. His hair was long and shiny and so black that it had hints of blue. Forge might have been attracted to him if Vince hadn't been straight. But after trying to end one marriage for the last eight months and going through hell, again and again, at this point in his life, Forge was planning to give up on men all together.

"What do we do from here?"

"We'll counteroffer, and I'll add all the legal points in our favor. At this point the law is on our side because it states very clearly for 'equitable division of the assets.' They should be close to even, not with one party deciding he wants it all because he's a greedy son of a bitch." Vince inhaled sharply. "Did I say that?" He placed his hand over his mouth, and Forge laughed for the first time in weeks. "Don't worry, I'll…."

"Can I see his offer again?" Forge asked. He was tempted to just tell Vince to take it. That way he could have this whole thing done and could move on with his life. One of the bones of contention was the house, especially since they still lived under the same roof. They hadn't slept in the same bed for eight months, not since Forge had kicked Granger's cheating ass out of the master bed, literally. Granger had had the gall, after the asshole's affair became public, to crawl into bed as normal. Forge had pushed him hard enough that Granger actually rolled onto the floor. A screaming match commenced, but it ended with Forge emptying Granger's closet by hauling everything to the guest room and dumping it in a pile on the floor. When Granger tried to stop him, Forge had used Granger's shoes as missiles.

Forge stopped his woolgathering and took the papers to look them over once again. "Go ahead with your plan." He handed the papers back, shaking his head. "But we have to bring this to an end, somehow. I need my life and my sanity back."

He had done his best not to allow the upheaval in his personal life to affect his work and friends, but he was finding that nearly impossible. As an interior designer for companies, he required a great deal of creativity, and that part of himself had been slowly dying throughout this ordeal. Forge knew he needed this to end so he could breathe again and maybe have a life that wasn't consumed with divorce proceedings, offers, counteroffers, and fights at home revolving around how Granger kept trying to hide assets.

"This will end. There is no doubt about that." Vince set the papers on his immaculately clean desk and stood.

Forge did the same and shook Vince's hand before leaving the office. He stopped to say hello to Vince's assistant, Gloria, before heading back to his office in downtown Milwaukee, lost in thought. Work was quickly becoming his sanctuary. Most days it was relatively quiet and he was able to think. But that was also a problem—his thoughts were consumed with his troubles with Granger.

"How did it go?" Rory asked, plopping into one of his desk chairs after closing the door. "What did Dickhead, Esquire, want now?" Rory was on his creative team and was bright and enthusiastic. He was also incredibly loyal and took delight in coming up with new and interesting lawyerly names for Granger. It was a source of amusement for both of them.

"More and more, it seems. Just when it looks like we're getting close, he changes his demands. I think this is a game for him. He doesn't need anything and has plenty of money, which he will still have when this is over. It's just an ego thing. Win at all costs—and I've about had it. Thankfully he's been on a business trip for the last few days and the house has been quiet. But that will change tonight." Forge wasn't looking forward to it.

"If you need anything, you know all you have to do is say something." Rory smiled the same smile he used when he wanted something. He had made little effort to hide the fact that he was interested in Forge, which Forge found flattering but nothing more.

"How about we talk about something else?" He needed something, anything else, to distract him.

"If we must," Rory said in an exaggerated manner, then gave him an update on where he was with all current projects for the design team that Forge headed. "The only problem right now is Midwest Bank. They still want to go with a variation of the same tired look they've had for twenty years, and it just makes them look out of step with the times. It's dated and makes the entire organization look worn out."

"I know. I've been giving that some thought. I have a meeting with a new client in fifteen minutes, but after that, let's sit down with the entire team and see what we can do to try to accomplish both goals. There has to be a way. We just need to find it." Forge hoped he sounded more confident than he felt.

"I don't know if that's possible, but we can try." Rory stood and left the office, giving Forge a few minutes to get ready for his meeting.

THE REST of the afternoon went more smoothly than Forge had thought it would. They developed a potential solution to their Midwest Bank problem, and Forge landed a new client that promised to be an interesting project. The thing was, he dreaded going home. Granger was going to be there, and the tension between them would have Forge's nerves on edge. Not for the first time, he

3

wondered how he and Granger had gotten to this point. They'd met twelve years earlier when Forge was twenty-four, and things had been great. They were both at the start of their careers and had been intent on taking on the world. They had built a life together, buying a house, getting married once it was legal, and working together a few times but mostly supporting each other.

Forge kept trying to figure out when things had gone wrong. Their passionate relationship had cooled somewhat over time, but they were still close, or had been, and they'd still been intimate even if they weren't humping like rabbits. They both worked long hours—maybe that had been it? Too much time at work and not enough time spent together at home, or taking the vacations they needed to reconnect on a regular basis. Maybe they both thought things were good until temptation stepped in front of one of them, and then things weren't so good anymore.

It hurt like hell that Granger had cheated on him with some kid he'd met at a club. Maybe if Granger had taken Forge to the club, the two of them could have had some fun together and things would have been different… maybe not.

Determined to put Granger out of his head for a while at least, Forge buried himself in brainstorming for his new client. When he finally sat back, the clock flashed 9:05 at him. Grabbing his computer case, Forge shut down his computer and pushed his chair away from his desk. He figured it was time to go home and face the music, the fighting… or, if he was lucky, the tense silence.

Everyone else from the team had left hours ago, and Forge said good night to the cleaning crew as he passed and headed for the exit. He rode the elevator down to the garage and went to his BMW sedan. He tried not to think about how it had been an anniversary gift from Granger almost five years before, when things between them were still bright. Forge got in, backed out, and exited the garage before making his way through city traffic to the freeway, then traveling north beyond the initial suburbs to River Hills.

HELL AND BACK

When they had decided to buy their house, Granger had been insistent it was going to be in the posh suburb. All the lots were two acres, and that meant huge, ostentatious homes—just what Granger had wanted. Forge exited the freeway and made his way home. He pulled into the long driveway along the side of the property and up to a house that was bigger than two people were ever going to need.

The lights were on everywhere, so Forge knew Granger was home. The man never met a light he could turn off behind him. Forge opened his door of the three-car garage and pulled inside, then closed it behind him. He got out and followed the light inside the silent house. "Granger!" Forge called before he could stop himself. He really shouldn't care where he was, and hell, Forge should be grateful for the quiet, make a quick dinner, and escape to his bedroom.

He set his case on the counter and walked through the downstairs rooms, expecting to hear Granger somewhere in the house, but he heard nothing. All was quiet. Forge went upstairs and wandered through the various rooms, including one that was empty except for a few boxes, because what did two people need with five bedrooms? They didn't, so they'd never used it. Granger's bedroom was neat and vacant, as were all the other rooms upstairs.

Forge wondered if he might have been wrong, but Granger's car had been in the garage, so he had to be home somewhere. Forge changed into more comfortable clothes and went back downstairs, then to the finished basement. They had built a huge media room there for parties and movies, but everything was dark. There was definitely something wrong. "Granger!" Forge yelled, his voice echoing through the cavernous entrance space. He returned to the kitchen, thinking about making something to eat, and noticed the sliding door that went out to the back deck was partially open.

"Granger?" he called more quietly as he pushed the door wide open and stepped out into the late-spring air. He inhaled, expecting to fill his nose with the scents of the flowering trees and shrubs that he'd planted all over the property. Sweetness filled his nose, but not quite what he was expecting. Forge walked to the far edge of the huge deck, to the very end of the circle of light, and looked out over the yard, but saw nothing. He returned to the kitchen and flipped on every switch, illuminating the backyard with a plethora of floods and landscape lighting.

Then he saw him, a figure, very familiar, lying on the grass, facedown. Forge gasped and willed his feet to move, but they remained planted where they were. Finally he got himself propelled down the deck stairs to the lawn and over to where Granger lay in a heap, covered in blood… so much blood. Forge turned away and lost whatever had been in his stomach, falling to his knees as he retched a few feet away from what was left of his husband. Even his military training as a medical logistics specialist, where he'd spent a lot of time in hospitals, hadn't prepared him for this.

Forge forced himself to turn and look at Granger. The body was covered in blood. What was left of his light blue shirt, mostly soaked with blood, was covered in holes. Someone had wanted to make sure Granger was not only dead, but ripped apart. For a second it reminded him of a scene from one of the Godfather movies.

Forge crumpled onto the ground, weeping softly for Granger. He cried for what they'd been to each other and for what might have been and had been snuffed out long before its time.

Once he was able to think again, he pulled his phone out of his pocket and called 911. "I need some help. My name is Forge Reynolds. My husband has been shot multiple times." He gave her the address and did his very best not to fall apart completely.

"Is he breathing?"

"No. I got home a few minutes ago and found him in the backyard. He's been shot, a lot of times, and…." He gasped and grew silent.

"Emergency services are on the way."

"Thank you, and we definitely need the police." It was probably a given from what he'd told her, but his mind was more than a little clouded at the moment.

6

"Don't worry, sir. We've alerted everyone, and they are already on their way." The operator continued to talk in a soothing voice, but he wasn't listening.

Sirens sounded in the distance, drawing closer. Forge went back inside and out the front door. Fire trucks, police, and an ambulance all arrived, filling his driveway. "They've arrived, thank you," Forge told the operator and hung up, then directed everyone out to the backyard.

An officer asked for Forge's information, and he rattled it off numbly. "Just wait in the living room," the policeman told him, and Forge did as instructed while everyone else traipsed through the house and out to the yard. The officer returned a few minutes later and sat on the edge of one of the chairs across from him. "I'm Officer Wilson. Can you tell me what happened?"

"I got home from work and found him in the backyard. I didn't know where he was at first, and it took me a while to find him. I knew Granger had to be home—his car was in the garage. I found the open patio door and turned on all the lights."

"Did you try to revive him?"

Forge shook his head. "He was covered in blood and full of holes. I got sick when I saw him." Forge tried to breathe evenly to keep down the possibility of getting sick again. "Then I called for help and all of you arrived."

"Isn't it late to get home from work?" Officer Wilson asked.

"Granger and I have been having problems. We're in the middle of a messy divorce… or at least we were. So coming home hasn't been very pleasant, and I work late quite a bit."

Officer Wilson nodded as he made notes. "Can anyone vouch for that?"

"Yes." Forge checked his watch. "I left the office forty minutes ago and said good night to the cleaning crew, Grant and his sister, Rhonda. They'll remember me." He provided the address where he worked, having nothing to hide.

"Did Granger have any enemies?"

7

"Probably. He was an attorney, combative and high-powered. He won a lot more cases than he lost, so I'm sure he made enemies of some sort. But I don't know anyone who'd want to kill him. He didn't do criminal work. He mostly represented companies or fought against them when that was the case. Sure, insurance companies loved and hated him, depending on what side of the case they were on, but I doubt they'd gun him down in the backyard." This whole thing didn't make any sense. He shook his head, unable to think of anything else to say.

"You said you were getting a divorce."

"Yes. We were married in 2014 when it became legal, and shortly afterward, things began falling apart, I guess. We filed about eight months ago."

"But you're both still living here?"

Forge shook his head. "Yes, we've both been living here, but in separate rooms. Granger is an attorney, so the divorce was another case he had to win. He cheated on me, and I kicked him out of our bedroom. It's been hard, but I didn't hurt him."

"I wasn't saying you did, but the more facts we have, the better." Officer Wilson continued making notes, and Forge wished he knew if Officer Wilson believed him or not. It worried him that they might think he'd done this when Forge had nothing to do with it. On television, ex-husbands and ex-wives got blamed for things all the time.

"I'm sure." Forge grew quiet since it seemed Officer Wilson might have run out of questions for now. But he had no illusions—there would be plenty more.

Another policeman appeared in the doorway, and Officer Wilson stood and walked over to him. They talked softly for a few seconds, and then Officer Wilson left. The other man sat down quietly. Forge knew he was being babysat, which was fine. He wasn't interested in being alone.

Forge dug his phone out of his pocket.

"What are you doing?"

"Making a call." He found the number in his contacts, and the call connected. "Vince, it's Forge. I need your help."

"I'm working on the papers now."

"I don't…. Look, I got home and found Granger shot in the backyard. I'm sure he's dead. The police are here right now and…."

"Jesus…. Okay, I'm on my way." Vince hung up, and Forge placed his phone on the coffee table.

"Mr. Reynolds," yet another officer said as he came into the room with Officer Wilson. The babysitter stayed where he was. "I'm Detective Coleridge." He looked at the others, and they retreated, leaving the two of them alone. "I understand you found the victim."

"Yes."

"Did you see or hear anything when you were out there?"

"No. I turned on the lights and saw Granger. I couldn't believe my eyes at first. I went to see if I could help him, but he wasn't moving and was full of holes and his skin was pale."

"Did you touch or move him in any way?"

"I didn't move him, and I don't think I touched him." Forge tried to remember even that short time ago. "No, I didn't touch him. With all that blood, I hadn't thought to." All he'd known was that Granger was gone for good now, and that last nugget of hope that resided down deep inside him had died. It was over for him and Granger—the marriage, the fighting, the love they'd once had. It was gone just like that. Forge leaned forward and cradled his head in his hands.

"Have you checked everywhere in the house?"

"Almost. Granger always left a trail of lights. Never turned off a switch in his life. He'd go to bed, close the door, and leave every light in the house turned on. If you wanted to know where he's been, you just followed the trail of lights." Forge didn't even look up. He was miserable, and this…. How did anyone deal with this?

"I think you need to come with me." Detective Coleridge stood, and Forge did as well, his legs shaky.

He followed him through the family room to Granger's office. The lights hadn't been on before, but they were now. From the doorway Forge saw the room had been tossed. He took a cautious step inside. Papers littered the floor, and the drawers to Granger's desk had been pulled out, the contents spilled onto the floor. All of Granger's books had been added to the pile, stripped off their perfectly neat shelves and thrown haphazardly. Pictures had been yanked off the walls and smashed on top of everything else, the chairs upended and cushions tossed aside.

"Jesus. They've been inside my house. Whoever the hell they are." Since Granger had been killed outside, it never occurred to him that the killers had been in the house.

"Do you know what they could be looking for?" Coleridge asked, but Forge shook his head.

"This was Granger's office, an extension of his work, and that meant confidentiality. Not that he kept work files in here—those rarely left the office. This was his sanctuary, where he went when he was bothered or wanted alone time." The sofa that had once been along the wall opposite the front windows was gone. Forge missed that old thing. When they'd first moved in, Granger had put their old living room sofa in his office.

Suddenly Forge was younger and he'd come into the office to bring Granger a mug of tea. It was winter and cold. Granger had looked up from what he'd been doing, heat in his gaze, and the mug had barely made it to the desk before they'd both toppled onto the sofa, tearing at each other's clothes….

"Sir?"

Forge blinked back to the present. Granger was gone, just like the sofa. There weren't ever going to be any more afternoons like that. Not that there had been recently. "I'm sorry. I haven't been in this room in months."

"Do you know what they were looking for? Is there a safe?"

"Yes. But if that's what they were hoping to find, they were way off. And it didn't hold anything that would be work-related. We kept personal valuables in it, like wills, deeds, and legal documents for the two of us. It's buried in the concrete basement floor and certainly isn't going anywhere short of them blasting it."

"Where's the computer?"

Forge carefully entered the room and walked around to the other side of the desk. He tugged on the front molding, and it lowered slightly. Then Forge found the lever under the desk on the right and moved it halfway, which shoved out a small block on the underside. Forge removed it and then pushed the molding down the rest of the way, revealing a finished shelf on rollers that slid out with the laptop sitting on top of it. "Granger loved puzzles. The shelves in the living room with the carved boxes?" He waited for Coleridge to nod. "They're all antique puzzle boxes. You have to know how to move things just right in order to open them. He collected them even as a kid. He loved the idea of a puzzle desk."

"Seems like a lot of work to me."

He smiled sadly. "Granger could unlock the desk in five seconds, in the pitch dark. He loved it." Forge stroked the smooth surface before pulling his hand back. "I'm sorry." He probably shouldn't touch anything he didn't need to.

"Sir, there's someone here to see Mr. Reynolds. He says he's his lawyer."

"We're going to need to take the computer," Coleridge said as Forge walked toward the door of the ransacked room.

Forge looked over his shoulder. "Of course. But good luck with it. Granger was a nut for electronic security, and if that laptop had anything to do with his work, it will be password protected and encrypted to within an inch of your life." He left the room and met Vince in the entrance hall. "Thank you for coming." He didn't know what else to do and was grateful when Vince wrapped him in a hug.

"I'm so sorry."

"Me too. Someone killed Granger, executed him in a hail of bullets it looks like, and they tore apart his office." Forge shivered hard. The entire evening felt surreal. "They were in the house." He paused as the coroner arrived and brought a gurney through. Forge shook as it hit him again that Granger was dead.

Vince pushed Forge toward the living room, then down to the couch, and sat next to him. "I'll talk to the police, but I doubt they can think you had anything to do with this."

"I gave them my alibi information. I was at work and had just come home." Thank God for building security cameras and the cleaning staff. "But what am I going to do? How can I be safe here?"

Vince nodded and reached into his bag, then rummaged for a few seconds before finding what he needed. "Call them. They provide security. I usually use them for female clients whose husbands, or sometimes abusers, don't want to let go."

Forge took the card.

When the officers returned, Vince stood and took charge. "Is there anything else we can help you with?"

"He lawyered up quickly," Coleridge observed snidely, making more notes.

"Actually he hasn't. I'm a friend, and I was his divorce attorney." Vince smiled the way a wolf might smile at a deer. "No one has said anything about him not cooperating to speak with you. However, the attitude is history. Once we know time of death, we should be able to prove he was nowhere near the house when Granger was killed, and he wants to help as much as he can so you catch who killed him. So lose the self-important behavior or the only way you'll be able to speak to him is through me, and that's the last thing you want during an investigation like this. Especially one that's going to make every newspaper in the state, by the looks of what's out front."

"Are there news people already?" Forge asked, looking toward the front of the house.

Vince pulled the curtains on the window. "Yes. They heard the calls on the scanner and scurried over. Just stay inside and don't talk to anyone. If you have to go out and are asked any questions, just say you have no comment. If they enter the property, call the police for trespassing."

Thank God Vince knew what to do about all this, because Forge was lost.

Coleridge cleared his throat. "I have just a few last things. If you're staying in the house, please refrain from going into the office. We're processing the scene now, but access tomorrow would also be good."

"Of course." The last thing Forge wanted was to go back in there.

"We've removed the body, and they're finishing work in the backyard."

"Do you have an approximate time of death?" Vince asked.

"Approximately six p.m.," Coleridge answered.

Forge thought for a minute. "So it's possible that they were already here when he got home. But then why not kill him in the house if he walked in on them?"

"It's fairly clear that he was shot outside. We've recovered bullets from the surrounding area. My guess is that he was already home, was lured outside, shot, and then the killers had all the time they needed. The lots here are big, so witnesses might be hard to find, and it's likely they used something to silence the shots. We'll know once the lab is able to analyze what we've found."

"How long will that take?"

"Unfortunately it can take a while. We need to send this in and then get in line with all the other cases from all the other jurisdictions. Of course, your friends in the news media have a way of moving things to the front of the line. I'll let you know what I can." Coleridge handed Forge a card. "Call me if you think of anything or come across anything."

"I will."

"The only thing I need to see before I leave is the safe you spoke about."

Forge got up and led Coleridge down to the basement. He moved a few boxes out of the corner to expose the top of the safe and worked the combination. Once it was unlocked, he pulled open the door. He reached inside and got out the papers they'd always kept in there. "Our wills." He was going to need Granger's, but he let Coleridge see it just to get that off the table.

Coleridge briefly looked over the documents that Forge withdrew. "You inherit everything."

Forge furrowed his brow. "Is that a surprise? We may have been separating, but as his husband, the majority of his assets would transfer to me anyway." Like the house they'd been fighting over, as well as all the other things Granger had worked to try to hide or transfer. All that hostility and fighting had been for nothing at all… on both their parts.

"Not at all. Is there anything in the safe that you don't expect?"

"No." He pulled out some of the trinkets and valuables that he and Granger had stored there. Jewelry from their families, and even some things they no longer wore. Envelopes containing a few letters and coins that had been given to him when he was a child. "There's nothing here."

"Okay. Then if they were looking for something, where would he hide it?" Coleridge asked.

"I don't know. As I said, Granger loved puzzles, so there might be a place to start on his computer. I just don't know. If I had an idea of what they wanted, then I might have an idea of what to look for." It was obvious Detective Coleridge didn't know what it was either. Forge packed everything back in the safe, closed the door, and locked it once again.

"Thank you." They climbed the stairs to join the others, who looked like they were packing up.

"I'll call if I think of anything, and I'm sure you'll be back to see me." Forge was running out of energy. He hadn't eaten since noon, and his lack of food and all the excitement was taking a toll.

Coleridge left with the others, and once the front door closed on the last of the police, Forge was alone with Vince.

Forge ran a hand over his face as he sat on the couch again. "What am I going to do?" There was no way he could go up to bed as though nothing had happened. What if the people who killed

14

Granger decided to come back? His first thought was to try to find a hotel or something.

"I already called my friends for you, and they're sending someone over. I didn't think being alone was a good idea. I've worked with them before, and they provide quality bodyguards. They understand security and how to protect people."

"But a stranger?" He wasn't sure how he felt about that. But then, staying in the house alone wasn't an option either.

"The man they're sending has worked with three of my clients over the years, and they all love him. This isn't something to worry about. He will understand what you're going through. He's former military, like you." Vince checked his watch. "I hate to leave you, but if I don't get back home, Carrie is going to rip my arms off."

"Your daughter is nine," Forge commented.

"True, but she has that tone that can make your spine want to crawl, and I promised her I'd be back before she went to bed." Vince chuckled. "Just be sure to lock all the doors and keep your phone close."

"Go on. I'll be fine until he arrives." Forge looked at the card again, then stood and saw Vince to the door. Once he was gone, Forge locked it and hurried through the house, making sure the doors and windows were secured. With that done Forge sat in the family room, turned on the television, and ignored it in favor of trying not to freak the hell out.

Now that the house was quiet and he was alone with his thoughts, Forge began to shake for a few seconds before calming himself. Granger was gone, murdered. Forge had no idea why all this was happening. But whatever the reason, he hoped they'd found what they wanted and would leave him alone now. He took a deep, steadying breath and tried to clear his mind. It didn't work, as all he kept seeing was Granger dead in the yard.

The doorbell rang, and Forge jumped half a mile. He was lucky he didn't put a hole in the ceiling. He went to answer it, but stopped before opening it, standing to the side against the wall. "Who is it?"

"Livingston Security," a deep voice answered. "Mr. Reynolds?"

"Yes." Forge unlocked the door, opened it, and stepped back to let the huge man inside. Reporters yelled questions at him in the brief moment it took for the man to step inside, but Forge tried to ignore them and the flashing of their cameras. He closed and locked the door once again. "I'm Forge Reynolds—" He turned and stopped dead in his tracks, looking into the deepest brown eyes he'd ever seen in his life. "Oh my God…." Forge couldn't help staring. He'd never expected to see those eyes or the man they were attached to again. "Gage? Gage Livingston?" Forge could hardly believe his eyes. Instantly he was transported back fifteen— no, seventeen—years to his days in the Army.

"I knew this had to be you. How many Forge Reynoldses are there in the world?" Gage turned and looked over the house while Forge shivered as a chill settled in the air. "We got a call that you needed some protection."

The additional shock nearly sent him to his knees. He hadn't ever expected to see Gage again, least of all on the worst day of his life. "My husband was killed in the backyard, and whoever did it trashed his office looking for something. I don't know if they found it, but… what if they didn't and they decide to come back?"

Gage nodded slowly. "Why don't you show me through the house so I can get an idea of what's where and any areas we'll need to secure?"

"Sure." Forge led the way, explaining what each room was and letting Gage look through them. He pulled out a small pad and made some notes. They only peered into the office, being careful not to disturb the security tape before moving on.

"Why were they only searching the office? Why not the entire house?" Gage asked. "It seems to me that if they were looking for something, they'd look everywhere."

"I have no idea, unless they knew whatever they wanted was in here. They didn't get his computer. The police have that." Forge explained about the desk, and Gage nodded. "There was no way they would have known it was in there unless Granger had specifically told them. So I'm not surprised they missed it."

"And you think if they didn't get what they wanted, they'll be back?"

"I don't know. Granger was murdered and his office ransacked. I don't know what to think." Forge held his head as a wave of dizziness came over him.

"When was the last time you ate?"

"Lunch."

Gage nodded. "Come on. Let's get you something to eat and maybe you'll feel better." He was all business, and part of Forge was grateful for it, while the other half was dying to ask the question he'd wanted to know for almost seventeen years, since he'd been transferred and Gage was getting ready to be sent home. God, that was so long ago, but Forge had been head over heels in love with Gage, and when he'd gotten settled, he'd written Gage at the address he'd given him. But he'd never gotten an answer. He'd thought Gage had loved him in return—he'd said he did—but there had never been a response. It broke his heart all those years ago.

Forge followed him into the kitchen, where Gage opened the refrigerator and pulled out a carton of orange juice. Forge motioned to where they kept the glasses. Gage opened the cabinet, grabbed one, poured him the juice, and slid the glass toward him on the granite countertop. "Drink that." He turned away, then pulled out sandwich things and nosed around for plates, making himself at home.

"How long have you been doing this kind of work?" Forge drank the juice, the sugar hitting him pretty quickly.

"I left the Army seventeen years ago, as you know. After a year or so of therapy and recovery, I needed something to do. A friend from Milwaukee convinced me to move here, and we started the business. I was looking for a way to be on my own, so I took his idea. I bought him out five years ago, and now I own and run it." Gage made sandwiches like he was dealing cards, then passed a plate over to Forge before taking a seat on the other side of the island. "What do you do?"

"I'm an interior designer for high-end clients, as well as corporate offices and work spaces. After I was done in the Army, I used my GI Bill to go to college." God, Forge remembered how hard that had been to start with. He'd never thought he had what it took to go to college, but a few years of being on his own and growing up had done him a world of good, and he'd been able to thrive. He ate the ham sandwich Gage had made him and felt better as soon as food hit his stomach.

"How long were you and Granger together?"

"Twelve and a half years. Ten happy ones, one tough one, followed by the last awful eight months, where we've fought over everything from the house to the damn furniture. He and I were in the midst of a split."

Gage set his sandwich back down on the plate. "I'm sorry."

Forge looked down at the counter, dangling his sandwich over his plate. "Granger cheated on me, but it was more than that. I can see where we'd been growing apart. Hindsight being twenty-twenty and all."

"And you both lived here… together?"

"Yes. He had his room and office, and I had my bedroom. We both worked all the time, probably to keep from seeing each other, because when we did, we tended to rehash all the arguments for the divorce. So instead of descending into a War of the Roses, we worked." Forge hadn't realized how pathetic his life had become until he talked about it that way.

"So you're still married?" Gage asked.

"Technically I'm a widower, and all the divorce fights and the hurt from his cheating came to nothing. I can still resent the son of a bitch, but he's gone…." Forge looked down at his sandwich again. "That hasn't even sunk in yet. And while I'm relieved, I'm not happy about it. Granger didn't deserve what happened to him." He lifted his gaze, the question he'd wanted to ask for nearly two decades on the tip of his tongue. But the look on Gage's face made it die out unasked.

Gage finished his sandwich and set the plate in the sink. "I'm going to check out the property and lighting. I suggest we turn on all the outdoor lights you have."

"Switches are right over there." Forge pointed, and Gage went over to turn them on as he peered outside.

"I'm going to go out and look things over. Lock the door behind me, and I'll knock when I want back in."

Gage slipped out, and Forge did as he asked, watching through the glass until Gage disappeared into the shadows at the edge of the yard. "Damn." Even knowing he was in the yard, Forge couldn't see him at all. He went back to finish his sandwich, feeling better just knowing Gage was out there.

He finished eating and added his plate to Gage's. He grabbed a soda and went into the family room once again. The television was still on, but he turned it off and sat, listening. As seconds ticked by, his anxiety ramped up. The refrigerator kicked on, and he started slightly before settling back into his chair. He'd been on edge since he found Granger dead, but this… the break-in. His nerves frayed a little more with every sound.

He yelped when Gage knocked on the back door, then went to open it. Forge's hands shook as he turned the bolt and let him in. Gage carried in a small bag and set it down. Thankfully, Gage closed and locked the door for him.

"Everything is fine outside. I didn't see anything. Go ahead and go on upstairs. Take a shower, let yourself relax a little, and then go to bed."

"Do you want me to show you to the guest room?"

"It's not necessary. I saw it when you showed me through the house. I'll only need a blanket if I can get one. You go on upstairs, and I'm going to stay down here. If you need anything, just yell. I'll hear you."

"Okay." Forge wasn't sure how well he was going to sleep, but he was dead on his feet and realized that everything around Granger's death was just beginning. This whole thing wasn't going to be a sprint, but more like a marathon, and he had to be able to go the distance. "I appreciate you coming on such short notice." His gaze caught Gage's, and for a second, he was right back in the hospital, sitting next to Gage's bed, listening and writing as Gage dictated a letter home to his family. Forge had spent many hours by that bed, reading Gage the letters he received and helping him write home. He'd also read him entire books during his off hours, and they'd often talked well into the night just so Gage wouldn't be alone when the pain got to be too much.

"It's no problem." Neither of them moved, and Forge barely heard Gage's response, his mind going in multiple directions. His memories pulled too hard at him.

Forge finally blinked out of his thoughts, turning away. "I'll get the blanket." He went up the stairs to the linen closet, brought one down, and handed it to Gage. Then he went back up to the master bathroom, undressed, and got into the shower.

The heat washed over him, his nearly cramping legs and arms finally letting go of the tension he'd been carrying for hours. However, his mind played emotional ping-pong, going back and forth between Granger's death and finding his body, to Gage being in his home, just downstairs. Forge tried not to wonder what would have happened if he'd come home earlier. He had little doubt that if he'd been home, they'd have killed him too. And the fact that he had Gage downstairs to protect him now was a comfort. A bodyguard was one thing, but Gage, after seventeen years…. Not that it mattered. Gage had walked away before…. But damn, those old feelings had roared back to life.

He finished showering, turned off the water, and dried off, checking himself in the mirror. Forge yawned and figured he might as well try to sleep. He pulled on a pair of boxers, walked into his bedroom, and climbed into bed after turning off the lights and pulling the curtains. Not that it did any good at all. He lay staring up at the high, coved ceiling, wondering if this whole thing had really happened. As much as he'd wanted to end his marriage to Granger, he wouldn't have wished this on him. And of course, now he felt so damned guilty for everything. Forge rolled over and closed his eyes. He needed to try to get some sleep somehow, but it looked as though it was going to be a long night.

CHAPTER 2

GAGE WENT through the house to turn out the interior lights before settling in the family room in front of the television with the volume on low, listening for anything out of the ordinary. One thing the Army had done a good job of training into him was patience. He could sit in a mostly empty house and listen for nothing for hours.

A lot of his jobs were hurry up and wait. This one had seemed like it would be more active. When the call had come in to the office, he'd been about to go off duty. Margie, his receptionist, had relayed who was calling and what they needed. That woman never seemed to sleep and had forwarded the office phone to her cell. There had been no one else available, so he'd sprung into action and hurried home to get a bag together. It wasn't until he'd been driving and Margie called to give him the particulars that he'd heard the name and nearly run off the road.

After all these years, to run into Forge again, and under these circumstances….

He turned toward the stairs and got up to make a round through the house, then checked outside just to ensure everything was quiet.

Forge Reynolds. Gage sat down, turned off the television, and retrieved his bag to pull out his iPad so he could read for a while. After a few minutes of reading the same page over and over, he set it aside, leaned back, and closed his eyes. Concentration wasn't something he had at the moment.

Almost instantly he was lying in a hospital bed.

He'd been hit with shrapnel, a ton of it if what he'd been told was true, and a piece had nicked his upper spine. He couldn't walk or use his arms at first. And he'd never forget the day a man, about his own age, sat in the chair next to his bed and picked up the pile of letters on his tray. They hadn't wanted to transport him in case it caused more damage, and his family couldn't visit him where he was, so old-fashioned communication was the best way.

"Would you like me to read them to you?" The man's voice had been mellow and gentle, at odds with most things in the Army.

"Please," he'd said softly. At least he'd been able to talk.

Forge had opened the first envelope and read Gage the letter from his mother, then a second one. The third envelope contained one from his mother and one from his dad, and Forge read both. Gage had been tired and fallen asleep, but when he woke, the man was still there. He picked up a pen and paper and asked if he wanted to write a letter. "My name's Specialist Forge Reynolds, by the way. I never did tell you."

"Staff Sergeant Livingston. Gage," he'd croaked, hating the way his voice sounded. He remembered feeling useless, helpless, and wanting to die. And when he'd dictated that first letter, all of it had come out in a burst of self-pity and loathing that Forge had faithfully written down, shown to him, and then ripped to shreds.

"Now, with that out of the way, what do you really want to tell your mother?" Forge understood that he'd needed to get that out, and Gage dictated a much better letter. Forge had mailed it for him and then came back every day, sometimes early in the morning and sometimes after his shift. Gage had looked forward to those visits and grew to need them as much as he needed air. When the pain hit once the swelling went down and he could move again, Forge had been there. The first time he'd held his hand, Gage thought his world had come to an end and his life, as he knew it, was now on a completely different path. Recuperation was hard, but he grew stronger, and then Forge said he was being transferred and they told him they were going to send him home.

Gage's eyes flew open as a bang sounded outside. He jumped to his feet, listening intently as it came again. He slipped out the back door into the night, keeping to the shadows. He easily made his way around the house, listening and hearing nothing for a while. He was about to go back inside when it sounded again. He made his way out front, shining his light toward the edge of the property toward the neighbor's drive, where he saw a trash can rolling around and pairs of eyes staring back at him. Raccoons. He was out chasing raccoons. He jogged back around the house to go inside.

Gage opened the door, and Forge jumped half a mile. He'd been standing in the kitchen with a baseball bat, in nothing but his boxers. Time had been good to him, and Gage turned away to avoid ogling the man. He still hadn't forgiven him yet, and seeing him that way wasn't doing a great deal for his professionalism. He remembered those pink nipples and that narrow waist. Hell, he even remembered the taste of his smooth, pale skin and how his lips were a gift from the very gods themselves. Forge's hair was a mess and in need of a haircut, but still looked as silky soft as he remembered. Gage raised his hands in front of himself. "It's all right."

"I heard something." Forge flipped on the lights.

"So did I. It was raccoons in the neighbor's garbage cans, having a feast." Gage figured it would be best to get the hell out of the room and away from a nearly naked Forge.

Forge lowered the bat a bit sheepishly, and put it away in the hall closet. Now that the crisis was over, his appetite apparently kicked in. He walked into the kitchen and dug in the refrigerator, his cotton-clad butt wagging slightly as he searched the lower shelves and came up with some fruit, which he then cut up. "I know I'm not going to get back to sleep again." He returned to the refrigerator and pulled out a beer. "Would you like one?"

"No. I'm trying to stay alert so if something happens, I can be ready."

Forge threw him a water instead and then turned to the coffeemaker, added coffee and water, and got it going.

"That will help, thanks."

"No problem." Forge showed him where the coffee and everything else was. "Just help yourself to anything you want." He grabbed his plate and left the kitchen.

Gage sighed with relief and took his water back to the family room. He got settled in his chair once again, switched on the television, and found a movie. Forge had all the channels, so Gage put on *42* and settled in to watch Jackie Robinson's story, getting some coffee halfway through to help stay awake.

Forge came into the room with a blanket and pillow, lay down on the sofa, and covered himself with the light blanket. "Is this okay?"

"Of course." It was his house, after all.

Gage did his best to watch the movie and keep one ear alerted to any possible threat. About halfway through, he got up to make a pass through the house and check the yard. By the time he returned, Forge was asleep on the sofa, his head resting on the pillow, lips parted gently. Gage had only gotten to see Forge sleep one other time, and that had been the night before his transfer and a few days before Gage was to be sent home. And he was just as angelic and beautiful, even if all the tension he was carrying was still there in his face and in the way he tossed and turned every few minutes. Gage turned the volume down a notch and continued watching the movie, hoping Forge would settle into a comfortable sleep.

The movie ended and Gage found another, then checked out the house again as quietly as possible. It was becoming clear that whoever had killed Granger and tossed his office wasn't coming back tonight for a second round. But that didn't mean he could let his guard down.

His second movie was nearly over and Forge was still asleep. The windows showed the sky lightening with the dawn, and Gage got up, poured himself another cup of coffee, and sat back in the chair. He finished the cup as the movie came to an end and closed his eyes, dozing off. He'd long ago mastered the ability to sleep with an ear to what was going on around him. Life in a combat zone would definitely do that for you.

Gage woke when he heard Forge coming down the stairs, but stayed where he was until the scent of food called to his empty stomach, along with the draw of fresh coffee. Nectar of the gods.

"I figured I should let you sleep a little since you were up all night." Forge brought in a plate with an english-muffin sandwich, as well as a fresh cup of coffee. He handed them to Gage, then went back to the kitchen. Forge returned with a plate of his own, sat down, and pulled the blanket over his bare legs.

"Did you sleep?"

"A little when I was down here with you. Up until then, not so much." Forge yawned. At least he'd pulled on a T-shirt and wasn't sitting around nearly naked and the epitome of temptation.

"I don't know if our friends are going to come back here. My honest opinion is that either they found what they wanted, or they didn't and they'll look elsewhere for it."

"Oh God." Forge set down his sandwich and put the plate on the coffee table. "I need to call his firm and tell them he's dead. He was one of the founding partners, and that will be a mess."

Gage swallowed, then cleared his throat. "Tell Vince and let him handle it. I know he's a divorce attorney, but he's probably done other things in his career and can help with any of the legalities. I've seen things like this before, and there's going to be a lot coming at you all at once. The police are going to want things from you, there will be demands placed on you by Granger's family, and you're going to need to arrange for a funeral."

"Granger's family…," Forge groaned. "I have to call them too. What do I say to them? They know we were splitting up. Hell, it's his father who had been urging Granger to give me as little as possible. The old bastard is a real piece of work. And I thought he liked me." He sighed, staring off into the distance.

"Call them and let them know what happened, and if you want, offer them the chance to plan the funeral. If they're going to be a problem, then hand the whole thing over to them and be done with it. If they want to do it, then they can pay for it too." Gage smiled, pleased that Forge nodded and some of the lines on his forehead lessened.

"How do you do that?" Forge asked. "Come up with suggestions like that and make them sound so reasonable? I never would have thought of that."

"Because you're the one who always wants to make everyone else happy." Gage remembered that vividly about Forge. The happiness of others always seemed to come first. It was his helping and caring nature that Gage had first fallen in love with. Too bad those feelings hadn't been truly shared, or hadn't been deep enough to last the separation.

Forge picked up his phone from the table and began making calls.

Gage finished his sandwich and coffee, then took the dishes into the kitchen to give Forge privacy. Gage used the time while Forge was on the phone to call into the office.

"Were you up all night?" Margie asked.

"Yes. I'm fine. Apparently there were news people here yesterday, but they seemed to have vanished with the police, so it was a very quiet night other than a family of raccoons." He yawned.

"You need to check your email when you have a chance, and there will be some invoices that need your approval. I'll put them on your desk and you can sign them in the next few days." Margie had the ability to look ahead, so when he was on an assignment, she was always able to give him as much time as possible.

"Thanks. Is there anything else?"

"Not right now."

"Hopefully things will move quickly here and this job will only be for a few days. I'll stop by as soon as I can." Gage poured another mug of coffee. "Call me if you need anything more."

"Get some rest." Margie was such a mother hen.

"I'll do my best." Gage ended the call and sipped from the mug. He had no idea when sleep was going to happen. He needed to be on top of his game, and his ability to do that was diminishing by the second.

Forge came in, looking even more shell-shocked than he had when Gage first arrived. "I called Granger's office, and they said the alarm had sounded last night. Security responded right away in force and so did the police. The robbers were scared off, and Granger's office is fine. I told them about Granger, and they're securing all of his cases and data. So that end of things is a dead end for them. Whoever the hell they are."

"Do you have a card for the detective in charge? I'll call him and make sure he has all the details. I take it his office is downtown?"

Forge nodded, pulled a card out of his wallet, and handed it to him. "I need to call Granger's parents."

"Do that now before they hear from someone else, and I'll call the detective."

Forge paled but dialed the number as he left the room once again.

Gage checked the number on the card and dialed. "Detective Coleridge, please."

"Speaking."

"My name is Gage Livingston, Livingston Security, and I'm providing protection for Forge Reynolds. He called Granger's downtown office this morning, and it seems they had an attempted break-in last night. Milwaukee police were apparently called, but it's probably related to Granger's death. We weren't sure if you'd been notified."

"I wasn't. Thank you." Coleridge sounded like Gage felt: as though he'd been up all night. "Is Mr. Reynolds available?"

"He's speaking with Granger's parents," Gage answered. "I can have him call or give him a message. Either that or you can call in a few minutes."

"I will. Thank you." Coleridge hung up, and Gage put his phone down. He hated this point in any investigation because it seemed as though nothing was happening, when in reality the police were exceedingly busy, verifying stories and processing evidence to try to put the pieces of what truly happened together.

Forge's voice rose, carrying in from the other room. "I don't know when the body will be released. The coroner has it and they'll be working with the police. As soon as I hear anything I'll let you know. … That's fine. You are welcome to make any arrangements you'd like. … Yes, I'm aware of that." Forge was becoming more and more agitated. "No, his being killed had nothing to do with me. They ripped apart his office here in the house, so they were looking for something. They also broke into his office downtown." The frantic tone had Gage's spine on edge. He'd been trying to give him privacy, but as loudly as Forge was speaking, that wasn't possible.

Gage hurried into the room, where Forge sat on the edge of the sofa, legs shaking. Gage heard a loud male voice coming through the phone. He reached out, and Forge blankly handed it to him. "This is Livingston Security," Gage said, shutting down the man he presumed was Granger's father. "This is a trying time for everyone, and yelling isn't the answer."

"He killed my son!"

"Forge most certainly did not. Now, you need to get yourself under control. Yes, Granger is gone and it's a shock, but taking it out on someone else isn't going to help either of you," Gage said in a firm, sharp tone.

"Granger's offices were broken into?"

"Yes. And it seems that Granger was targeted specifically. I suspect the police will be contacting you, but Forge wanted to be the one to tell you what happened. Now, are you going to kill the messenger or listen to what he has to say?" Gage would end the call now if Granger's father didn't calm down.

A woman answered him. "This is just such a shock for us." She sounded strained and had clearly been holding back tears.

"I understand that, ma'am, and I'm very sorry for your loss. But things like this are hard on everyone. Don't take it out on each other. Leave the hatred and vitriol for the men who killed him.

They deserve it, not Forge." He handed the phone back and sat down. He'd been hired to protect Forge, and he'd protect him from his in-laws as well.

"It's okay, Mom. I know this is hard." Forge sniffed and began to cry silently, his shoulders rising and falling. "I know. It's been hard for months." He wiped his eyes and sniffed again. "Anyway, I'll call as soon as I know anything." He hung up and leaned back on the sofa. "That sucked. I never thought I'd have to call people to explain that Granger… or anyone… had been killed. Let alone tell his parents."

"What about your parents?" Gage asked, thinking that maybe they could help support Forge.

"Mom passed eleven years ago, and Dad just last year."

"They must have been young?"

"Dad and Mom would be nearly eighty now." Forge leaned back. "I was their miracle baby. At least that's what they said. Mom had always been told she couldn't have children. They'd made their peace with it and had planned their lives around the two of them. They were even talking about buying a place in Florida for vacations and eventual retirement, and then at thirty-nine…." He smiled. "Mom thought the change of life was coming on early, but when she saw the doctor…." Forge wiped his eyes. "She always told me the doctor's expression was a mixture of joy and shock when he told her she was pregnant." He got up and went to the bookshelves on the left side of the huge television, then returned with an old album and opened it. "That's Mom and me."

Gage chuckled at the picture of the very pregnant, dainty woman who looked like a grape ready to pop.

"She spent two months on near complete bed rest, and when I came, it was so fast, I was born at home with an EMT helping Mom. And that was it. I was healthy, and both of them were thrilled beyond belief."

The house phone rang, and Forge got up to answer it. Gage paged through the album, looking at the pictures of Forge as a kid, then in middle and high school. The album ended with a few pictures of Forge in the Army… and the last picture stopped Gage in his tracks.

A bang had Gage on his feet in seconds and over to where Forge stood, phone receiver on the floor. At first he thought Forge had just dropped it. Gage bent to retrieve it, and as the line was dead, he hung it back up. "It's okay."

Forge shook his head violently. "That was…."

"What?" Gage froze, hardly breathing.

"Them."

"Don't touch anything." Gage pulled out his phone and redialed the detective's number.

"Yeah?"

"Detective, I think you need to come back to Forge Reynolds's home. He got a phone call. He's in shock at the moment. They called a landline, so you should be able to get the last number called."

"What did they say?" he asked, and Gage turned to Forge, placing his phone on speaker.

"They said that I still had what they wanted and that I'd better produce the files before they come after me, and it won't be clean like it was for Granger." Forge barely held it together, he was shaking so badly. "It was an electronic voice so I don't know anything more, but it was enough to scare the shit out of me."

"What's the number they called in on?" When Forge gave it to him, Coleridge said, "I'll be there in ten minutes. Keep everything locked." He disconnected, and Gage guided Forge back to the family room and down onto the sofa.

"I guess that answers the question about whether they found what they wanted or not," Gage said, taking Forge's hand.

"Yeah, but what the hell could they be looking for and how am I supposed to find it?"

"They said they wanted the files…," Gage mused aloud. "But what kind and where the hell did Granger put them?"

He shrugged. "Who knows? I suspect that whatever they want is probably locked in Granger's computer. Those are the only files I can think of. The police have it, so it isn't likely I'm going to get it back any time soon."

"True. But what if they aren't those kinds of files?" If they could find whatever it was and hand them over, Forge might be safer. Of course, the police finding out who was behind this was the easiest way to get them off the street and to keep Forge safe. "Just answer the detective's questions as best you can."

The sat in silence until the doorbell rang, its Westminster chime bouncing through the house. Gage got up and let two officers in. "Detective Coleridge, I'm Gage Livingston." They shook hands.

"Your reputation precedes you," Coleridge said.

"I hope that's good."

Gage didn't get an answer.

"This is Officer Wilson."

Gage nodded. "Forge is in the family room." He lowered his voice and leaned in. "This has been a terrible day for him."

"We understand." Coleridge went in with Wilson, and Gage followed.

Forge was hanging up the phone. "I called the office and told them I wouldn't be in. They had already heard about Granger on the news." He didn't get up, setting the phone on the table once more, looking like a dog who'd been beaten over and over again.

Coleridge sat in the chair across from Forge and was quiet for a few seconds. "Tell me about the phone call."

Forge relayed what had been said again, almost word for word. Gage was willing to bet he could hear it playing over and over in his head.

"Do you have any idea what files they want?"

"No. There aren't any paper files here at home. They would be on his computer or in his office. Granger was a nut about client confidentiality and security. Attorney-client privilege was a religion to him. He'd never take the chance that their information would end up in someone else's hands... even mine."

Coleridge appeared thoughtful. "There were locking drawers on his desk."

"Yes, and they weren't locked because he never used them." Forge looked about ready to shatter into a million pieces, and Gage shifted closer, touching his shoulder for support. "Did you find anything on his computer?"

Coleridge sighed. "No. Do you know his password? Or anything to help us get inside?"

Forge shook his head. "The man was security crazy. Even if I knew the password, most of the files would be encrypted and you'd have to have the codes to read them. So if something is on that computer, it's lost to the world. That was the only way Granger would ever have brought anything home." He turned to Gage. "I don't think every attorney does that, so I'm wondering now what he had to hide."

"That's what we're wondering too," Coleridge said with what Gage read as complete honesty. "There's a motive behind this death. It isn't a crime of passion, but either hatred or someone sending a message. It's too early for the autopsy results."

"Did you get anything about the phone call?"

"There's a display on the phone. We could try the call-back function. Most people don't think of disabling it any longer because everything is cell phones," Gage said. "They could have withheld the number, but you have to specifically block that feature."

"Old school. I like it." Coleridge and Officer Wilson went to the phone and seemed pleased when they returned. "We have a number. Now we need to trace it to see what it is." Coleridge smiled, obviously happy, and sat on the couch.

"Did you have other questions while you're here?" Forge asked.

Coleridge consulted his notes and thought a moment. "Did Granger keep to a routine?"

Forge shook his head. "Not especially. He did what he needed to for his clients. Sometimes he was home early, and other nights he didn't get home until ten. The last few years he worked all the time, more once we started the separation."

"What caused the breakup?"

"I caught Granger with another man. Typical story. He wasn't expecting me home, and I found him. Kicked his twink's ass to the curb, then chewed out Granger for days. I know now that the cheating was a symptom of bigger problems, but I hadn't recognized them. As I said, we'd been fighting over what seems like stupid stuff until…." Forge lowered his head and held it in his hands. "I didn't have anything to do with this."

"We don't believe you did. Everything you've told us has checked out. But please let us know if you think of anything else."

"Oh…." Forge raised his head. "How long do you think it will be before they release Granger's body? I spoke to his parents in Chicago, and they'd like to plan the funeral and things. I told them it would be a while."

"It will. I'm not sure how long we'll need it, but I'll see what I can do." Coleridge stood, and Gage walked him and Officer Wilson to the door.

Once they were gone, Gage sat next to Forge, the urge to help him nearly overpowering.

"Oh my God, I forgot about that," Forge said as he picked up the photo album, looking at the picture of the two of them. Gage was propped up in bed with pillows, and Forge sat next to him. "The picture, not the day. One of the other specialists took that two days before you shipped out. He had it developed, and I carried it with me until I got home. Mom kept this album, and I gave it to her. She must have stuck it in here." He set the album on his lap.

Gage didn't understand. "Why?"

"Why what? Carry the picture?"

Gage nodded his answer, a lump forming in his throat.

Forge shrugged. "It was all I had of you."

"Then why didn't you write? I was shipped home, and you said you were being transferred so you were going to write." There, he'd said it. "I was sent home and spent months in therapy and rehab, going through a hell I can't even describe. There were days when every step hurt, and at night I'd nearly cry myself to sleep. Every day when my parents came to visit, they'd bring my mail, and I waited to hear from you. At night sometimes, when the pain was at its worst, I used to think of you coming to see me, and all the agony would be worth it because I'd be able to walk to you." Gage took in a huge breath, the anger leaving his voice as suddenly as it had come. "But no letter ever came."

"What the hell?" Forge set the album on the coffee table. "I wrote to you, at least six times, every other day for almost two weeks until the first one came back, and then they all did." He jumped to his feet and raced up the stairs. Gage heard him fumble around and then race down the stairs, returning with an old red shoebox. It was tattered and had probably been in the back or bottom of a closet for years. Forge opened the box and unceremoniously dumped the contents on the coffee table.

Gage picked up a pin and held it in his palm. "Combat Action Badge."

"Yeah. I got it for rescuing a wounded soldier, one of the men in my unit, while we were under fire." Forge pushed aside the various papers until he pulled out a small set of envelopes and handed them over.

"You kept them?" Gage held the letters as though they were precious.

"I don't know if I meant to or not. I threw them in the box with the rest of my Army things and pretty much forgot about them. I wasn't even sure they were here." Forge sat back, gesturing at the papers. "See, I wrote to you."

Gage looked at the envelopes. Five were still sealed, but one had been opened and reclosed with yellowed Scotch tape. They all had Return To Sender written in bold black ink across the address.

"I never got them." He read the address, which appeared correct. "My God." He carefully opened the first letter, the paper somewhat yellowed also. He read the letter and then put it back in the envelope. He turned it over again and swore under his breath.

"What?"

"How dare they!" Gage swore again as anger welled inside. He could see his mother sitting at the kitchen table, opening this letter, reading it, and then resealing the envelope and sending it back. The controlling old bat.

"Who?" Forge asked, looking bewildered.

"My parents. My mother always figured that any mail that came to the house was hers to read if she wanted to. As a kid, I learned to make sure I got the mail whenever possible, especially as I got older." He breathed deeply and released it. "This is beautiful." Gage held the pages tightly in his fingers as the realization of what had been taken away washed over him. As he thought about it, the notion that his mother had sent back the letters solidified. "And while this isn't explicit, my mother would certainly have gotten a pretty good idea about us."

Forge reached out, and Gage handed him the pages. He read the note and gave it back, sighing. "I thought I was being so careful, and yet there it is in black and white if you know what to look for."

Gage nodded. "I wish I'd have gotten these." Not that it changed a great deal now. He hadn't gotten the letters, and his life, as well as Forge's, had gone in a completely different direction. Gage had recovered and refused to let the injury stop him. He'd worked his body back into peak shape once the hurt had shifted to anger and determination. Forge's letters had gone astray, he'd met Granger, and they'd had a life together.

"Me too. Everything wasn't all bad for Granger and me. We had some good years. Of course, things didn't turn out the way I expected at the beginning. He was charming and driven, with lots of energy. We had fun together until the work took off for both of us, and then we…." Forge began putting things back in the

36

box. "It doesn't matter now. What happened is done." He finished gathering the last of the mementos, and Gage tried to hand back the letters. "You keep them. They were meant to go to you." Forge took the box and left the room.

Gage watched every sway of Forge's hips until he was out of sight. He sat back in the chair, the letters resting on his lap, and closed his eyes. The lack of sleep was catching up with him. It had to be. Forge was a client, and he should not, under any circumstances, be having the salacious thoughts running through his head about any client. But he couldn't help it. Suddenly he was seventeen years younger, behind a locked door, and while everything wasn't fully functional yet, the important parts worked, and Forge had shown him just how well and what getting better would truly mean. They'd only had one night of intimacy and passion, though their attraction had simmered for weeks. Then Gage was on his way home to his parents and their stifling sense of propriety, with a future of recovery and pain, looking forward to… something that would never happen.

GAGE DOZED off, needing to sleep some if he was to be alert and protect Forge. No matter how tired he was, Gage had learned long ago to remain alert, so it was surprising when he woke and found a blanket thrown over him and Forge sitting on the sofa with several boxes from the shelf lined up on the coffee table. He sat up. "What are you doing?"

"Trying to remember how to open these. They're Granger's puzzle boxes, and each one opens differently. Granger could work all of them in mere seconds, and he showed me how to open them." Forge turned a box over and then upright again, tugging out a small piece of the decoration, which allowed another piece to move, and finally the end slid off. He peered inside and closed the lid. "Nothing." He put the box back on the shelf and returned to the table.

"How many have you opened?"

"That was the fourth one. It's taking a while for me to figure them out again." Forge picked up another and worked it quickly. "Some I remember." He smiled and shook his head, closing the box once again and adding it to those on the shelf. "I don't expect to find anything. These were objects of art to Granger, not utilitarian items." He continued opening the two dozen or so small puzzle boxes, and Gage stood, leaving the blanket behind, and made his rounds of the house once again and checked out the yard in the daylight.

The police had marked where Granger had fallen, and Gage was able to follow the path of activity to where bullets were found, as well as to where the shooter had likely stood toward the side of the backyard. He placed his feet near where the shooter had been, turning to look around. It was a perfect spot. Two trees sheltered the area perfectly from the other houses in the distance. Berms around both of them added to the cover and would diminish the effects of any sound.

"What are you doing?" Forge asked as he strode across the yard.

"Get back inside," Gage told him, the hairs on the back of his neck standing on end. "Please go." He had long ago learned to trust his instincts, and they were screaming at him. Following Forge, Gage turned toward the house, walked briskly to the back door, closed it, and pulled the curtains.

"What's going on? It's broad daylight."

"And easy for someone to see what they're shooting at. These people don't care about night or day."

"Oh." Forge sat in one of the kitchen chairs, shaking.

"And I think I was being watched." Gage wished he could shake the intense notion that he'd been so exposed and had eyes on him.

"I hate that feeling." Forge sat still, his hands flat on the table. "This whole thing sucks. Not only is Granger dead, but I feel like a prisoner in my own house." He stood a little unsteadily, went back into the family room, and began to work more of those puzzle boxes.

Gage called in to his office. "It's me. I need some things." He dictated a list. "I'll stop by the office today and pick them up. I'm going to bring the client with me."

"Very good. Give me a few hours, and I'll get everything together for you."

"Thanks, Margie." He ended the call and looked around the room, wondering to himself. People had been in this house looking for something. They'd obviously had some time. He wondered if, in addition to tossing the office, they might have left a few gifts behind.

"Forge, who lives in the houses over there?" When Forge joined him in the kitchen, Gage pointed, then indicated for Forge to sit at the table. Gage dug through the pantry until he found tea and made him a mug, hoping it would be more soothing than another round of full-strength coffee.

"The one next door is the Harpers. He's a doctor at Children's Hospital, and they have three kids. Two boys and a girl. I've only seen them a few times. The one in back…." Forge sipped his tea. "Right now I understand they're in Europe for the summer. Granger was pissed as hell when they built that fake Victorian monstrosity and put it so far back on the lot behind us. We have two acres, but they're mostly to the west. The backyard is huge, but it was once a field, so the trees haven't had a chance to grow up to block the view completely. That's why there's the line of trees to the north. A few were already there, and we added a number of them that will eventually block the view and make the yard more private. Why?"

"Nothing you need to worry about." Gage had a pretty good idea just from his instinct, which had never been wrong before, that the poor people in Europe were going to come home to find that someone had been using their house. He left and placed a call once he was out of the room. "Harv, you up for some fun?" He spoke as softly as possible.

"What kind?"

"Empty house that I think is being used for spying on a client. Want to take a look?" Gage knew Harv couldn't say no. He was a thief at heart—well, an honest one. But he loved to see what he could get away with, and he was damn good about getting into places without anyone knowing he'd come and gone.

"When and where?" Harv asked with delight in his voice.

Gage gave him Forge's address. "Drive something no one will notice, and after dark we'll pay a little visit to the empty house that I think isn't so empty." Harv agreed, and Gage hung up, smiling. "Forge, I have to pick up some things at my office," he said when he returned to the kitchen.

"Okay. I'll lock the doors and—"

Gage shook his head. "You're going to come with me. I can watch over you best if you're along with me. We can get anything you need."

"What about the house?"

"You're more important than the house, and I don't want to leave you alone, but there are some things I need."

"Okay. Let me shower and change. Give me ten minutes." Forge took his tea along with him, and Gage watched him go, knowing he shouldn't.

Something inside his mind had shifted. The resentment he'd carried about Forge not writing had evaporated. When it came to Forge and this job, the one thing that had kept him professional was the thought that Forge hadn't really loved him, and that not communicating had been his cowardly way out. But Forge wasn't a coward and he had cared, a great deal.

"Do you want to clean up?" Forge asked when he came down in what Gage was certain was just a light blue robe, that enticing strip of chest and belly visible from where the knot had loosened while walking.

"Thank you. I think I will." He grabbed his bag along the way, and Forge led him to a huge bathroom with towels all laid out for him.

"I'll be ready when you are." Forge left him alone, and Gage stripped and set out his change of clean clothes before starting the water. He showered quickly because he couldn't hear anything while he was in under the water, then jumped out and opened the door just to make sure Forge was okay. The door across the hall was open, and Gage saw Forge clearly through it. He closed the bathroom door, dried off, and dressed without wasting a motion. His hair still damp, he gathered his things in his bag and left the bathroom. He found Forge working the last of the puzzle boxes.

"They were all empty except the last one." He showed Gage a picture. "I got that one for Granger as a gift years ago, and he put this picture in it." Forge's eyes were wet, and Gage wondered just how over Granger Forge really was. An act of immediate and final violence could have many effects, including forgiveness and rose-colored glasses. "We were so young then." Forge smiled and put the picture back inside, then closed the box. "At least we know there was nothing in any of them to help."

Trying to keep his own feelings in check, Gage asked, "Can you think of anywhere else to look?"

"The safe-deposit box?" Forge asked. "I grabbed the keys from Granger's hiding place when I was dressing."

"Was this the box for both of you or just him?"

"I'm not sure. Granger had me sign some papers for one a few years ago. I never saw the keys, but I knew where he put them. Maybe he figured I forgot about it, or he could have closed it and these are to something else. All we can do is see what he left." Forge dropped the keys into his pocket, and Gage got them ready to go.

He set up a tell at each of the outside doors so he'd know if anyone tried to get in, then ushered Forge out to his car and took off, driving as fast as he dared and taking as many extra turns as possible. He didn't think they were being tailed, but he wanted to be sure. He drove to a low white utilitarian building in an industrial area closer to the city, pulled the car directly inside, and closed the overhead doors. "Best way to hide from anyone."

Gage climbed out of his dark blue Camry and slammed the door, the sound bouncing off the walls in the otherwise empty space. He grabbed his bag from the back seat, then waited for Forge before showing him through to the office. Margie sat behind her desk, phone headset resting on her head.

"I have everything you asked for." She took a call as she pointed to the bag. "Yes. I'll let him know." She typed as she spoke, probably sending him an email about one of the details another of his security people was on. "Glad it's going well and that they want you for two more weeks." She disconnected the call and looked up expectantly.

"Margie, this is Forge Reynolds," Gage said, going through the bag she'd put together for him. Then he walked into his office to check his email while Forge and Margie talked in the outer area.

"Is he always that brusque?"

"Oh no. He's just busy and wants to clear as much of his desk as he can in the next few minutes."

Nothing fazed Margie. She knew how much he valued her, and when he was in a hurry, she let him be.

Gage opened his email and went through the list, answering what he could quickly and putting the rest into his to-do folder for later. He checked on his staff, pleased with their overall progress. Then he stopped. "Margie. Is this true?" He read the email she'd just sent. "Two more weeks? I have another detail for him."

Walking over to the doorway, she said, "They're paying time and a half, so I figured that would make it worth it. I've already got Marcus ready to step in to take the other job. So we're covered."

Gage smiled at her. "What would I do without you?"

"Probably spend more time in the office and climb the walls within two weeks. I know what you love, and that's why you hired me—so you can continue to do what you love." She leaned closer. "You need to get back out there before your client starts getting restless. If I was a little younger and he was a little older…." She waggled her eyebrows.

He smirked. It was his turn to put one over on her. "You'd also need to change genders."

"How do you know?" She turned to peer out to the reception area and then back at Gage. "Is he… the one?"

"One what?"

Margie rolled her eyes with the efficiency and effectiveness of any teenager. "The one who got away. The one who stole your heart and… basically the one who turned you into a relationships-don't-last kind of guy." She took a step into his office. "He is, isn't he? Don't think I haven't learned a lot about you in the five years I've worked here. And I saw the way you looked at him, like he was a buffet lunch and you were starving."

"Don't be dramatic. You don't do it very well." Now it was his turn to roll his eyes.

"I knew something happened a long time ago."

Gage stared bullets at her. "Harv has a big mouth." He should have known.

She grinned even more. "Great. Now I know who to pump for information."

"Remind me never to play poker with you." He went back to his computer, and Forge wandered in to sit in one of the chairs. "You're perfectly safe here. We're surrounded by enough surveillance and sensors that if a mouse tried to get in, we'd know before it got halfway across the parking lot." Gage motioned to the door to the side of the office. "There's a suite with a bathroom and rest quarters through there, also a television and some comfortable chairs. There's more here to do than I thought, and…."

"I think I'll watch TV if that's okay." Forge looked tired, and Gage hoped he could relax. Hell, he'd like to do the same thing, and maybe if he finished up some work, he could lie down for a while. Tonight was shaping up to be busy.

FOR THE next hour, Gage worked his way through emails and invoice approvals. Then he shut down his computer and went in search of Forge, who he found sound asleep in front of the television.

Smiling at the turn of events, he went to get a blanket. He covered Forge and got one for himself, then lay on the sofa, falling to sleep within seconds. This was the one place he knew he could relax, where both of them were absolutely safe.

Gage wasn't sure how long he slept, but when he woke, Forge was still out, if the snoring was any indication. "Man, you could wake the dead."

"Huh?" Forge startled, then yawned. "Oh. Yeah, I know. Granger used to give me grief about it. When we were first together, he'd rouse me by curling close and holding me. He said I'd settle right back to sleep and be quiet. Eventually it got to him asking me to roll over. Then him nudging me, and eventually he'd leave the bed." Forge sat up and hung his head. "I know now I was really stupid."

"No. You were going on with your life. Maybe you and Granger needed to talk more often."

"That was another issue. Granger talked all day long for work, so he was pretty quiet when he got home. He never wanted to talk about much other than what we were having for dinner or if there was some problem he needed to deal with. Mostly he either sat in his office or in front of the television." Forge picked at a stray string on his clothes, not meeting Gage's eye. "Things were falling apart right in front of my eyes, and I didn't do anything about it."

"He still should have talked to you instead of shutting you out." Gage sat up and blinked a few times, feeling better and more alert now that he'd gotten some rest. "I think we need to move on."

"It would be nice if we could just stay here for a while. It's peaceful and safe."

"Then relax for a while." Gage checked his watch. There was no need to hurry. "I have something I need to do tonight. You're welcome to stay here."

Forge sat back once again. "It's nice here, but I want to go home. It probably sounds stupid, but it's where I'm most comfortable." He groaned and ran his fingers through his hair. "This is going to sound dumb, but being at the house makes me feel closer to Granger in a weird way, and I think that's what I need right now."

"Okay…." Gage shrugged, hoping for nonchalance.

"I don't have any illusions about how things were between us, but I need to be able to end things and say goodbye. I expected that to happen in a courtroom or from across a negotiating table, and instead it's going to be at a funeral."

"Then do you want to get going?" Gage asked, wanting things to be as normal for Forge as possible.

"In a little while." Forge returned his attention to the television.

Gage found himself watching Forge instead of the movie. For some reason, Forge's inner strength surprised him. It shouldn't have, given his history. Gage truthfully wasn't sure he would be handling the events since yesterday with as much grace and fortitude as Forge was if their situations had been reversed.

After another movie and a little more rest, Gage packed up the blankets, loaded the equipment Margie had gathered for him, and left the office. They stopped at the store for provisions, then returned to Forge's house, where he drove by and parked up the road.

"What are you doing?" Forge asked.

Gage ignored him, grabbing his phone instead, and called Harv. "Where are you?"

"At the house. It's clear."

Gage pulled his car into the driveway, and Forge used the remote on his key ring to open one of the overhead doors. Though full dark had fallen, they went inside quickly, with Gage acting as a shield as best he could to cover Forge. He returned for his bag and closed the door, then continued into the house. Gage hurried through the inside, checking his indicators, which were all still in place, confirming what Harv had said.

"Where's your friend?" Forge asked as he nervously sat at the kitchen table. "Is it always going to be like this? Checking the house and being afraid whenever I come home?"

"Harv is around, and he'll make his presence known if we need him or if he sees something. Right now it's best he stay out of sight and be an extra set of eyes and ears." Gage set down the equipment. "As for your last question. Yes, that's to be expected. Being cautious is prudent, and being afraid… fear helps keep us on our toes." He placed his hands on Forge's shoulders, amazed at how right it felt to protect and care for him. Gage could try to deny his feelings, but it was getting more and more difficult. Forge's distress called out to him and touched that place deep inside that Gage had forgotten existed. "I'm going to do everything I can to help keep you safe. You need to stay away from the doors and windows, and keep the curtains closed." He squeezed his fingers slightly as his own nervous energy ramped up. Gage preferred to channel that energy into productivity. "I have some sensors that I'm going to install on the doors and windows to try to give us a heads-up should anyone try to pay us an unexpected visit. And this evening, Harv and I are going to do some reconnaissance. He's also going to be installing an alarm system to help give us some advanced warning."

Forge placed his hand on top of one of Gage's, and heat ran from his fingers through Gage's arm to his body, settling in his gut and racing out in all directions. He stifled a groan and did his best not to shake as energy built to near unbearable levels. A simple touch was enough to send his entire body into overdrive, and his dick to aching something fierce. For a second Gage was back in the hospital, basking in the warmth and care of Forge's gaze, and he wished, more than anything, that he could change what happened. But the past was always out of reach, and had to be accepted and dealt with. Gage knew it was impossible to go back.

He leaned closer and kept his voice low. "I need to get some things done."

Forge nodded and pulled his hand away. Gage missed it the way a drowning man misses air.

46

CHAPTER 3

FORGE MADE coffee and sat in the kitchen as Gage went about his tasks, letting him do what he needed to. Dark clouds settled around Forge, and he let them gather. He needed to deal with the loss, as well as the ultimate change to his life. He knew it wasn't as simple as thinking about it and working through everything in a few hours. He sat at the table where he and Granger had eaten a lot of meals together before things between them had completely fallen apart.

"You know, it's okay to mourn for him, for what the two of you had," Gage said gently.

Forge looked up. "How do you know what I'm thinking?"

"It isn't rocket science, and I've seen a lot of grief and confusion. Shit happens to all of us, and sometimes what we get is manure, piled on crap, wrapped in shit. You deal with it as best you can and move on." Gage refilled his mug, and Forge followed his movements.

Gage was dressed all in black and looked completely badass and sexy as all hell. Suddenly the clouds around him parted a little and some light shone through. "What are you doing?"

"Some reconnaissance with Harv. I need you to stay here in the house with everything locked up. Don't open any of the outside doors or the first-floor windows while I'm gone unless you need me or something happens. I have them temporarily sensored, and I'll get a message on my cell phone and come right back."

"Is Harv still out there?"

"Yes." Gage peered out the side curtain briefly and let it slide back. He pulled out his phone, scanning through what Forge thought was a text. He answered it with a grin and slid the phone back into his pocket. "Please just stay here and keep the doors closed and locked."

Forge tried to keep the concern out of his expression, but Gage must have seen it. He paused at the door, looking at him before returning to where Forge sat. "I know you know what you're doing," Forge said.

"Yes." Gage leaned closer, his face inches from Forge's. "If you need anything, open an outside window and then run and hide. I'll get a notification and come right back. But don't open the door for anyone other than me, no matter who they say they are or what they want." Gage didn't move, his lips so close, their eyes boring into each other.

Forge was scared to move in case the spell between them broke. Gage inched closer and paused once again. Forge tilted his head, parting his lips, but a scrape outside the kitchen patio door startled him. He pulled back, instantly on alert and berating himself for not taking advantage of the opportunity.

"That's Harv." Gage took his hand. "Remember what I said." He swallowed, and Forge tried to make his mind work. He managed to nod once, and then Gage was gone out the door, closing it, and Forge locked it right behind him, letting the curtains fall closed.

Forge went into the family room and sat in his favorite chair. He thought of trying to watch television, but he was too nerved up, wondering what Gage was up to. He figured Gage had purposely not told him what the plan was. Still, Forge had an idea that it involved his neighbor's house.

In a way he wished Gage had asked him to come along. Forge had military training and he could defend himself, though his skills were nearly decades old and he hadn't kept them honed the way Gage had. Forge shook his head and picked up his phone, holding it in his hand just so it would be ready in case he needed it.

Silence reigned around him, and Forge needed something to do. Sitting in the house, waiting for whatever could happen, was driving him crazy. He intended to do what Gage had asked, but instead stood and went to one of the windows in the rear spare bedroom, where he could see the house behind his. He turned off the inside lights and peered outside. The lights in the back lit the yard, but he could see past that to the other house, which loomed large in the darkness, only a backdoor light as a clear beacon giving away its location. Other than that, he saw nothing. Hell, what did he expect, people running hither and yon across the yard in fear as Gage chased them all down? Forge chuckled as he let the curtains fall back into place and returned to the family room.

After another ten minutes, a soft knock sounded on the back door. He went and checked who it was before letting a grinning Gage inside. "Did you find what you expected?"

"Yes. It seems your neighbors are going to come home to a mess. But they're gone. Someone had been staying there, probably to watch over this house. From the looks of it, they'd been there for a few days and left about the time of Granger's shooting."

"So they were watching us?" Forge shivered.

Another knock, and Gage let in a small, wiry man who seemed about a hundred twenty pounds. A good, stiff breeze could probably blow him away. Like Gage, he was dressed all in black. As he pulled away the outer layer of clothes, his handsomeness emerged, along with a head of black hair plastered to his scalp and a T-shirt completely soaked through.

"I think so. But it seems like a lot to go through just to kill someone." Gage turned to the other man. "Forge, this is Harv."

"I'll be going in a few minutes." He shook Forge's hand, then stepped away.

"Do you need somewhere to clean up?" Forge asked.

"No. I just need to go. I've been out there in the humidity for a good part of the day. Thank you, though." Harv turned to Gage. "I checked the house for any signals that might indicate a bug and found none. You might want to check for any record and return devices, but other than that, you're clean." He paused. "Oh, and once I leave, I'll make an anonymous report to the police about the house in back."

"All right. I appreciate the help." Gage let Harv out the door once again, and he disappeared into the night. Gage relocked the door.

"Did you break into my neighbor's house? What is going on here?" Forge asked, confused.

"We didn't break anything, and no one will know we were there. But we needed to check things out," Gage told him. "A small group of people, probably two or three, set up shop in your neighbor's house in the rooms where they could look into your house, probably with telescopes and other equipment. It also wouldn't surprise me if they used parabolic listening equipment to find out what was being said over here. But like I said, if they'd wanted Granger dead, they'd just have killed him."

Forge shivered at the thought that he and Granger had been watched. Their lives, such as they were, had been exposed to strangers, people watching them. A chill ran up his spine that hung there. "Does this help figure out what in the hell they want?" Someone had killed Granger, and if he thought finding out who'd done it was going to be a walk in the park, he'd just had his eyes opened.

"No. They were probably trying to get it from Granger before they killed him, and he told them to take a hike." Gage sat at the table, and Forge stood to make them each a sandwich because he had to have something to do. "All this is only a theory. Unlike in the movies, I didn't find any papers or some clue that will lead to an explanation of everything that's happening."

"So let's say Granger was doing something at work or had a client who was outside the law…. Like a gangster?"

"It's possible. They have lawyers, lots of them, and they pay very well and reward loyalty. But what if Granger betrayed them?" Gage shook his head. "We're going off on a tangent. We don't know very much about what's behind this. The best way to find out is to try to locate whatever these files are."

"If I had to guess, I'd still say they're something on his computer. But we'll never know. The police will keep his computer until they've gone through everything on it."

"Then tomorrow we'll check out the safe-deposit box, and we can check with the police on the disposition of Granger's body. Hopefully they'll know something more."

Without really hearing any more of what Gage said, Forge stood and walked to the basement door. He went down the stairs to the safe and opened it, then pulled everything out and transferred it to a box, which he brought back upstairs and placed on the table before sitting back down.

Gage gave him an odd look. "Just eat your sandwich and we can go through all this." Gage sounded slightly like Forge's dad when he tried to soothe him.

Forge nodded but didn't touch his food. The clouds were back, darker and more oppressive than before. "I have to find it," he said, pulling out each item and looking it over before setting it aside again.

"But you don't know what to look for."

"Not really." God, he wished this was all over and he could return to his life. Forge reached for an envelope and stopped, tears welling. Things were never going to be the same, no matter what he did.

Gage gently touched his hand, and he let the envelope fall to the table. "Eat something."

Forge nodded and picked up the sandwich with his other hand, turning the one Gage was holding and wrapping his fingers with Gage's. This probably wasn't a good idea, but instantly his mind went back to happier times when he'd sat next to Gage's bed, celebrating the return of movement to the very hand he was holding.

A bang from the lawn made him jump, and Forge squeezed Gage's hand harder. He closed his eyes and prayed that if the people who murdered Granger had come back, they got it over with quickly.

Gage let go and stood to go to the window. He peered around the edge of the curtains and then turned back inside. "A family of deer have decided to spend the evening, and they've knocked over one of the metal planters." He returned and sat back down, pulling out the phone. He finished what he was doing and then took Forge's hand once again.

"I remember doing this under your blankets so no one in the hospital would see us." Forge had been so young and stupid. They'd have been kicked out of the service if they'd been caught. "But that was a long time ago."

"And sometimes it seems like yesterday." Gage leaned a little closer, and this time Forge didn't hesitate to close the gap between them. Forge closed his eyes and for a second was transported back to their first kiss, which had been sweet and tentative. Now Forge pressed closer, heat rising fast, and Gage slid his fingers through Forge's hair, pulling him closer. The table was in the way, and Forge wished he could push it from them. But Gage gentled the kiss, caressing his lips ever so slightly with his tongue before backing away, tugging on Forge's lower lip. "I waited seventeen years to do that again."

"Me too," Forge whispered. "Sometimes I used to think… no, wonder what would happen if things had turned out differently between us. Would we have gotten married the way Granger and I did, and would we have grown apart? In my memories you were always twenty-one and so damned beautiful."

Gage smiled gently. "But you remember me in the bed, crippled."

Forge shook his head. "No. What I remember is your eyes and the way you made me laugh. Even when you could move only your head, you still brought me joy." He took Gage's hand and kissed it. "I remember one night, I'd been reading to you for a few weeks, and you fell asleep. Your hand was outside of the covers, so I took it and gently placed it underneath so you wouldn't get cold, and you squeezed it. Not much, but you did. It was the first time your hand moved, and it was because of my touch."

Gage's eyes widened and then his expression softened. For a second Forge saw some of what they used to share in the hospital. "How come you never told me?"

"Because the next day, you could move your hand, then the other one, and the whole hospital was excited. I couldn't tell anyone that I'd been holding your hand, so I kept that memory to myself. It was mine, and after you got sent home and my letters went unanswered, I held that memory tighter."

Gage sat still, and Forge let the spell that had settled hang in the air for a bit, then turned his attention to his sandwich. Gage got up to make some herbal tea, then brought him a mug. Forge finished eating, his attention focused on the papers from the safe. He'd already gotten the will, but as he went through things, he found other documents he was going to need, like powers of attorney and the title to Granger's car.

"What are all these?" Gage held up a blue box.

"Oh." Forge smiled, set the papers to the side, and pulled out what looked like small jewelry boxes. "They're coins. Granger used to buy them for me when we first got together. They aren't real tender, at least not in this country, but they are silver. They commemorated some of the initial milestones in our relationship." He opened one and handed it to Gage. "They were something he used to do. At the time, we were both trying to figure things out, and Granger said they were an investment of sorts. The silver would always be worth something." He closed the case and picked up another. The coin rattled inside, and Forge opened the case to put it back on its slot. When he did, a small black item tumbled out onto the floor. Forge reached down to pick it up. "What's this?" He set what looked like a piece of plastic back on the table.

"It's a drive." Gage lifted it, looking it over. It was tiny and plain black, maybe an inch in length. "Could this be what you're looking for?" he asked with excitement. He pushed back his chair and returned with a small laptop. Gage started it up and inserted the drive. He turned the screen and sat next to Forge as they both waited for the computer to recognize the drive and bring up the list of contents.

"I don't think this is what we're looking for," Forge said as he glanced over the file names. "It seems to be the electronic version of the wills and other documents." That was Granger being thorough. Forge continued looking through the contents of the safe and found the envelope the drive had originally been in. It had come open, but God knows how it had gotten into the case. "I don't see anything else." Forge packed everything up again, then carried it all downstairs and placed it back in the safe, locked it up, and covered it once more.

When he came back upstairs, Gage was going through the files. "Just double-checking. It's getting late. In the morning we'll go to the bank to see about the safe-deposit box. Things are getting away from me a little…."

"It's all right. Tomorrow is fine." He was tired and wound up tight as a drum. Forge hadn't slept well last night, and he wasn't sure how well he was going to sleep tonight either. All he wanted was this whole thing to be over so he could pick up the pieces of his life and move forward.

Forge finished the last of his sandwich and drank his tea, then put the dishes in the dishwasher and got it running. He figured Gage would make himself comfortable where he needed to. "If you need anything—"

"Look at this," Gage said, still at the computer. "The last file is empty. Or rather, it opens to a blank page."

Forge went to peer over Gage's shoulder at the screen.

Gage closed the file and reopened it to be sure, but it was blank. "It was called Granger&Forge. I thought it might have contained something he wanted to remember, but there's nothing here." He closed the file and removed the drive to hand it back.

Forge took it, wondering where he was going to put it. He wasn't interested in going back down to the safe, so he went into the living room and grabbed Granger's most complex puzzle box and put it inside. "Bedding is in the linen closet upstairs if you need anything."

"I'll figure it out."

Forge hesitated at the bottom of the stairs, turning toward where Gage sat at the table. He wanted to go back and kiss Gage good night. Hell, he wanted to kiss him hello, good night, and where the hell have you been for the last seventeen years… all at the same time. But he didn't dare, and Gage seemed to have slipped back into professional mode, so he wasn't sure if the act would be welcomed, no matter how steamy the earlier one had been.

He climbed the stairs and went to his room, where he undressed, cleaned up, and used the toilet in the master bathroom before climbing under the covers and trying to sleep. He heard Gage move through the house for a few minutes, and then everything grew quiet. Forge calmed down, feeling safe knowing that Gage was downstairs looking out for him. Still, sleep didn't come. He was too far away, and after an hour, Forge got out of bed and opened the door. He could barely hear the television downstairs. He grabbed the light blanket off the bed, wrapped himself in it, and went down the stairs.

Gage sat in the chair, a mug of coffee next to him, watching an action movie. He looked up at Forge's arrival. "Are you okay?"

"Can't sleep." Forge sat on the sofa, intending to curl up, but he was too warm, so he lay down with the blanket over his legs, turned toward the television.

"Jesus," Gage said under his breath.

Forge ignored it because he wasn't sure if he was meant to hear it or not. A house exploded on the television, and he closed his eyes, trying to relax. He wasn't really interested in the movie as much as he didn't want to be alone. He turned away from the TV and met Gage's heated gaze. The temperature rose higher, and Forge pushed the blanket farther off his legs.

He sat still as Gage stood and crossed the room in a few strides to stand over him. He didn't take his eyes off him for a split second, afraid to blink in case this was his imagination. Gage sat on the edge of the cushion near his hips, an arm resting on the back of the sofa.

"You know, you're like temptation personified." Gage stayed where he was. "I…." He swallowed visibly. "Do you have any idea what you're doing to me? Your husband was killed, and no matter what happened in the past, or the fact that you did send letters years ago, I can't…." He kept halting and ran his hand through his hair. Forge was quickly realizing that was how Gage released his nervous energy.

He reached up and took Gage's hand. "Stop that or you'll rub yourself bald, and I like your hair."

Gage rolled his eyes. "Okay. But it doesn't change anything."

"My marriage has been over, except for the yelling, for months." Forge tugged at Gage's hand, bringing him closer. "Granger was the one who stepped out of the marriage. I never did. I was loyal until the end, and…."

"How long has it been?" Gage whispered, coming ever closer, the energy between them increasing with each inch Gage narrowed between them until Forge was afraid he was going to fly to pieces if Gage didn't touch him.

"Since Granger had someone else, I refused to be with him. If he was getting it somewhere else, then he wasn't going to be with me. Who knows what he could bring home." Forge had trusted him, but look what the hell happened. After that, he'd been tested for everything imaginable and stayed the hell away. A cheater will cheat no matter what.

"I'd never do that," Gage told him. "I haven't had the kind of relationship you had. This job and my life were never conducive to one. But when I was with someone, it was only him." He inched still closer, and Forge wrapped his arms around his neck, pulling them together, unable to take any more.

Forge devoured Gage with pent-up passion, banked on hold for seventeen years, combined with the want and need of eight or nine months of abstinence. When Gage worked his arms under him, holding him tightly, Forge's skin came alive. He hadn't realized just how starved he'd been for the touch of someone he cared about until he had it. Now he didn't want it to end.

"Gage," Forge breathed when they pulled apart.

"Is this really okay? I don't want to push or rush you."

Forge closed his eyes and shook his head. "I've waited a long time for this. I know you were waiting to hear from me, but I was doing the same, near the front lines in a field hospital, hoping to hear from you. I thought you didn't care for me. Now that I know that wasn't the truth, I want to make up for the years we lost." He slammed his lips to Gage's, throwing all those years of wishing into the kiss, which Gage returned. The fire between them was all-consuming, a conflagration burning away time and distance until it was just them right here, right now. Nothing else mattered, and Forge was determined to make everything he could of the opportunity while Gage was in his arms.

"Oh, Jesus," Gage murmured, pulling away and heaving for air as Forge did the same, then took his lips once again. He tugged at the hem of Gage's shirt, needing to feel his powerful chest against his body. His memories had mellowed and softened into a warm sepia, but he needed full-on technicolor, with all its bright vividness and intensity. Forge needed to feel alive and unrejected. To be wanted and cared for with the depth and enthusiasm only youth could bring. And regardless of the time that had passed, Gage gave that to him, in nearly overwhelming waves of heat.

Forge pulled at the fabric, yanking it upward, but instead of Gage's shirt giving way, the crisp sound of a tear filled the room as the fabric ripped. Gage didn't pause his kisses, and soon Forge held the remnants of Gage's shirt, which he tossed away as he arched up against him. That was what he needed.

Gage tightened his hold, stroking his back. This time, when Gage broke the kiss, Forge lolled his head back, so Gage licked down his throat to the base of his neck, then worried a spot at the base of his shoulder until Forge nearly went to pieces.

"Dammit." He clung to Gage, hoping he didn't explode.

Gage pulled away, standing back, and Forge blinked up at him, wondering if he'd done something wrong. He blinked again as Gage stood over him, his gaze traveling up Gage's flat, heaving stomach to his chiseled chest. "Come on. You have about ten seconds to get off the sofa and up to your bed, or I'm going to flip you over and take you right here." Gage's voice was deep as hell and getting lower with each and every word. He heaved for breath and took one single step back, pointing. Forge thought about just how much he cared where they were together and realized a bed would be much better. He stood, the blanket falling away, his dick tenting his boxers, and Gage growled.

Forge hurried out of the room and reached the base of the stairs before heavy footsteps sounded behind him. He took off and got to the bedroom before Gage tackled him onto the mattress. Somehow Forge rolled over, his boxers making it off his legs and onto the floor. Then Gage swallowed him. Forge could have sworn he hovered over the bed in complete, passionate bliss as wet, molten heat surrounded him, gripping and tugging at him. He clutched at Gage, pressing his hips upward, needing all that Gage could give, getting so much more than he ever expected. "Holy hell!"

"You can say that again." Gage pulled off and gripped Forge's cock, stroking hard. "I don't remember you being this big."

Some smart comment about the bigger, the better or something had worked up in his mind, but it flew from his head as Gage took him once more. Nothing else mattered. Forge lay back on the bed, his arms over his head, giving himself to whatever delightful deviltry Gage had in mind. Instinct from deep in his brain said Gage knew what he needed and would give him the greatest joy he could remember. Second by second, each touch and lick only added to that impression. "Gage." Forge brought the heel of his hand to his teeth and bit down, trying to keep hold of himself. His control cracked, then broke a minute later, and his release surged into Gage with an unstoppable force that left him panting and seeing stars that outnumbered those in the night sky. And in those moments of complete clarity, he realized just how much had been missing from his life and what he wanted going forward forever.

"Are you still with me?" Gage asked quietly.

"Oh God." Forge stretched to tug Gage to where he could kiss him, tasting himself on Gage's tongue.

"You are so amazingly hot like this. Laid out on the bed for me." Gage straightened, stepping back, and Forge stared with rapt attention as Gage toed off his shoes and shucked his pants and boxers. Once he stood very proudly naked in front of him, Forge licked his lips. Gage was as stunning as Forge remembered, maybe more so. When they were together then, Gage hadn't been at his best, but he certainly was now.

Forge guided Gage closer to the bed, then rolled over and shifted until he lay on his belly right in front of Gage. He lifted his head, at perfect cock level, and slid his lips around Gage.

Gage shook as Forge took him deeper, cupping his balls gently as he bobbed his head. Forge loved cock sucking and adored the feel of Gage's cockhead across his tongue. Gage rocked back and forth slightly, and Forge closed his eyes, letting the sensation roll over him. This was amazing and something he'd waited a long time for.

When Gage pulled away, Forge opened his eyes, wondering what was happening. Gage climbed onto the bed, guiding Forge to the pillow and settling between his legs. "Are you ready for me?"

"I've been ready for a long time." Forge swallowed hard and pointed to the bedside table, hoping the supplies were still there. At first Granger had begged to come back, so Forge had gotten condoms in case things progressed down that path. But they never did, and thankfully the supplies were still there.

Gage pulled out the strip of condoms and a bottle of lube, setting them near the bed before turning his pulse-racing gaze on Forge, who had no idea how he was going to survive what was coming. He hated to admit it, even to himself, but he'd wondered in his heart of hearts what it would be like to have Gage back in his life, and now it was happening. Gage lifted Forge's legs and leaned over him, kissing hard as he slicked his fingers and breached him for the first time. Forge's hiss turned to a sigh as his body got used to the invasion, then slowly morphed into craving it. He needed more, and Gage seemed all too happy to oblige.

"I'm ready."

"You sure?" Gage's eyes sparkled with excitement.

"I've been ready since I met you again, and before that… I think I've missed you more than I can put into words." He braced himself as Gage slid on a condom and then back into position. He pushed into Forge's body with a stretch and burn that left Forge speechless and made his head spin.

"Damn, you're tight around me." Gage continued slowly pressing forward, and Forge placed his hand on Gage's hip to stop him. He needed a second to breathe and get used to what was happening. Soon he was aching for more, so he nodded, and Gage sank deeper.

"So big," Forge groaned, gripping the bedding He needed something to keep him grounded, because each second his head grew lighter and he was sure he was going to fly away at any minute. Instead, Gage held him, kissing him deeply and stroking his chest and down his belly before gripping his now-reawakened cock. Forge had no idea how much more he was going to be able to take as Gage slowly rocked back and forth, dragging his cock over that electric spot inside him that sent shocks running from head to toe.

"I've been missing you for so long, I think it's become part of my very being," Gage admitted, and Forge nodded. He'd lost track of the other half of his soul and now it was back, right here with him.

"I… know… just… how… you… feel…." Words were too hard, and forming coherent thoughts became harder and harder, so he completely gave up and rode wave upon wave of Gage's passion. Forge had no choice but to give himself over to what Gage wanted. Somehow he knew it was what he wanted as well.

"Not going to last...." Gage moaned, and Forge nodded once again, digging his fingers into the bedding to hold on for dear life.

"I don't want you to," Forge said, and he moved right along with Gage. "Just let go and let me watch you." He needed to see Gage release and watch his face as passion consumed him. Forge managed to hold off his own excitement long enough for Gage to still, his mouth falling open and his eyes widening as he throbbed inside him, coming hard and heaving for breath. He pulled Gage down onto him, holding him tightly, letting him float through the release. "Damn, that was gorgeous."

"So are you."

Forge closed his eyes and let the adrenaline pump through him. Gage kissed him, gently this time, and he closed his eyes, listening to Gage breathe quietly. He wanted to rest and probably fall asleep, but the hair on his arms stood on end and he strained to hear.

"What is it?" Gage asked.

"There's someone in the house...."

At that moment Gage's cell phone dinged, and he fished it out of his pants, took a glance at it, and yanked on his jeans. "Go to the bathroom, lock the door, and stay there." Gage opened the bedroom door and quietly slipped out.

Forge found his boxers and pulled them on, then did exactly as Gage told him. He hunkered down in the bathroom and listened for any signs of distress even as his nerves ramped up even more.

A thud vibrated through the house, and Forge stood and had his hand on the knob, ready to leave and find out what was going on. All he could imagine was Gage hurt on the floor. The waiting around was driving him crazy. He cracked the door and listened. He heard a slam and then everything grew quiet once again.

"Forge," Gage called.

Forge left the bathroom and slowly went down the stairs. "What happened?"

"He didn't get far," Gage said, though he stayed by the door, not meeting Forge's eye. "Picked the lock. The guy was sloppy, and you heard him. My alarm went off when he opened the door, and I met him just as he'd taken a few steps inside."

"What did you do?" Forge stayed close to the stairs, ready to run if necessary.

"Kicked him in the gut, and he took off." Gage locked the door and reset the alarm. Then he made a call to Coleridge, and Forge listened as he explained what had happened. "Yes, we're both safe, and I have the house secured. … I see. … Well, thank you. … No, I didn't see anything. The house was dark and I got a good kick in. I may have cracked some of his ribs before he took off, heading west. … All right…." Gage hung up and finally looked up to where Forge stood. "They're going to be right over."

"Crap," Forge groaned. He'd had enough of the police and everyone else. "I wish I could find whatever it is these guys want. I'd give it to them just so they'd leave me the hell alone." He lowered his gaze and turned to go back up the stairs. "Do you think I should put on jeans… or maybe I could slip into a tuxedo to be questioned by the police again."

Gage shrugged. "I think anything other than just your boxers will do." He followed him up, and they dressed quickly. "Coleridge said it's been a busy night in our neighborhood and asked if I'd made any forays. It seems your neighbor's house was being used as a lookout post." Gage winked, and Forge wondered how he could be so cheerful. Gage gave a rueful smile and shrugged again. "Make the best of a bad situation."

By the time they returned downstairs, the police had arrived. Forge let Coleridge in, gesturing to the living room, and explained what had happened. Then Gage, who had stayed on the other side of the room, answered questions, both about the break-in, and, of course, Coleridge wondered if Gage had anything to do with an anonymous tip they'd received regarding the house behind Forge's.

"Gage didn't make any phone calls to you as far as I know," Forge said honestly, without breaking a smile. "Have you made any progress figuring out who shot Granger?" He figured it was time to turn the tables. He was getting tired of answering everyone else's questions.

"We're running down some leads right now. But it's looking as though multiple people are involved, and we're centering around his work. But the law firm isn't providing any information on his clients, and unless we can get more information, we can't go to a judge to get a search warrant for his office files." Coleridge was clearly tired, the case taking its toll. Or it could have been that it was nearly midnight and he looked like he'd been working for the entire day and wasn't done yet.

"We kept searching here for possible locations for those files they referred to, but haven't found anything. And I'm guessing they haven't either if they came back," Forge said as the rush began to wear off and he yawned broadly. "I found the keys to the safe-deposit box."

"Okay. I'll be over in the morning, and we can go see if there's anything inside." There was a hint of passionate expectation in Coleridge's voice. "I'll be here at a little before nine."

"Just meet us at the bank downtown," Gage offered. "We'll bring the keys and see if the account is still open, and if it is, find out what's inside. Honestly, what we're afraid of is, if the account is still open and Forge isn't on the account."

"That's why I'm there. I can call to get a warrant to open it. Legally, since Granger is dead and you're his beneficiary, what's inside belongs to you, so your cooperation will mean we can get a warrant quickly." Now Detective Coleridge sounded excited. The man certainly could go from down to up in a few seconds. "We'll meet you at the bank at nine."

"Perfect," Forge said. He was willing to do anything necessary to wrap this up. Maybe then he could have his life back. Forge turned to Gage and wondered if, when this was all over, he'd stick around or if Gage would be off on another case, and if it was going to be another seventeen years before he saw him again.

"All right. Call if anything else happens, and I'll see you in the morning." Detective Coleridge left, and Forge leaned back in his chair, his eyes already falling closed.

"Go on up to bed," Gage told him. "I'm going to stay down here." He left the room, and Forge shivered in the air-conditioning. At some point he'd expected to feel alone. After all, Granger had been killed, and even though they'd been in the midst of separating, they'd still been together for over ten years. Up until that moment when Gage walked away, Forge hadn't been alone—Gage had been there. But his leaving the room left Forge very much alone, like the physical distance between them mirrored the mental distance Forge had seen widening in Gage's eyes when Forge first reached the bottom of the stairs.

Forge yawned and went to his room. He was exhausted and needed some sleep. But once he was in bed, Gage's scent surrounded him and the tang of sex lingered in the room. There was no way Forge was going to be able to sleep. He rolled over and closed his eyes, trying like hell not to fall apart and failing. Everything from the last two days caught up to him, and he couldn't hold it inside no matter how hard he tried.

CHAPTER 4

GUILT TOTALLY sucked, but that's where Gage was at, and the damned crap wasn't going away no matter how many times he tried to give himself a break. He'd let himself be led up to Forge's room and gotten completely lost in him. His mind and body totally focused on Forge, which had nearly been disastrous for both of them. It couldn't happen again. Gage was here to do a job. Forge was paying him to protect him, not take him to bed and fuck the living daylights out of him. What the hell had he been thinking, having sex when he was supposed to have been working? To top it off, Forge had been the one to alert him to the intruder before his own equipment and senses had kicked in.

He got out of the chair and went to the kitchen to pour a huge mug of extrastrong coffee. He carried it through the house, making sure all the doors and windows were secure and peering outside just to check that nothing looked out of the ordinary. Gage was too restless to sit back down, so he wandered from room to room, quietly padding over the carpeting and prowling like a restless tiger. No matter what he did or how he tried to justify what happened, he wasn't able to forget the fact that his desire for Forge had, in effect, put him in danger. And to top it off, if he'd been on guard, he might have been able to apprehend the guy and they could have gotten something useful out of him.

"Shit… shit… shit…," he groaned under his breath. "You're fucking better than that." Maybe he'd be better off turning this particular job over to Harv or one of the other guys and stepping back. He was obviously too close to Forge to think and act the way he should.

After a while, Gage climbed the stairs and went to Forge's room. The door was open, with just enough light for him to see

Forge lying on his side, rolled away from him, hopefully asleep and getting some much-needed rest. That's how it should be—Forge asleep in his own bed and Gage staying awake to protect him. He turned and went back downstairs to check the house once more before gulping his coffee to stay awake.

He heard a creak on the stairs and froze.

"Are you trying to wear a hole in my carpet?" Forge asked as he joined him in the living room, once again in nothing but a pair of boxers—walking, talking temptation.

"I just need to stay alert in case they make yet another attempt on you and the house." Gage yawned, trying his damned best to stop it and failing miserably.

"You have all the alarms set, and if anyone tried to get in, your phone will set off enough noise to wake the dead, right?" Forge took his hand as Gage nodded. "Then come get some sleep. You dead on your feet isn't doing anyone any good." Forge tugged him toward the stairs. When Gage resisted, Forge tugged harder. "Don't argue."

"God, you're bossy." Gage smiled crookedly with a glint in his eyes.

"That's right, I'm the boss, the one you're protecting, so I say you need to do that from much closer. I've been lying up there listening to you and wondering what the hell happened. Then I heard you pacing like a caged wolf and I figured it out… at least I hope so. If it's guilt that's bothering you, stop it now!" Forge halted and glared at him. "It takes two to tango, and if there's any blame or guilt to go around, then we share it equally." He smiled. "Just like with Nurse Ratched. Remember her?"

Gage smirked. "God, yes. Claire Goodwin. That woman had the coldest hands, and she could make a simple injection feel like cutting off a limb. We used to play the best tricks on her."

"She hated them, of course, but that was the fun."

"Remember her plant?" Gage asked and Forge howled. "That damned poinsettia that only got worse- and worse-looking as she tried to make it last through to Christmas." They'd both gotten so sick of seeing it rot away outside the door of Gage's room that they kept a fresh plant in secret and started supergluing green leaves on her old one each day so she thought it was returning to life. Gage shook his head. "She never did figure out who was behind that."

"Nope," Forge said, "but she accused you and me. I remember reminding her that you were paralyzed and there was no way you could have done it."

"Then I swore it didn't happen during the day when you worked because I would have seen it. She tried to work it out and eventually threw the damn thing away." Gage smiled so broadly, his cheeks ached.

"Exactly. I'd have taken the heat if necessary, and so would you, so let go of whatever you're thinking. We have a puzzle to solve, and we aren't going to do it on a few hours' sleep." Forge tugged him up the stairs and into his room, leaving the door open. "Do you have your phone?"

"Yes." Gage liked this side of Forge. So far, Gage had seen him take a back seat to what Gage instructed, but this was nice. A man who knew what he wanted.

"Then put it on the table beside the bed, get undressed, and let's try to get some sleep."

"You know, I'm a professional and I shouldn't be sleeping with my client, even if he is someone I knew years ago and wished I never lost touch with." Gage sighed. This was getting complicated.

"I'm not paying for you to sleep with me. That isn't what this is. You're here to protect me and do what you need to in order to keep me safe." Forge turned around, his hands on his hips. "But dammit, I just found you again, and if you think I'm going to let you worry or guilt yourself into being stupid, you can think again." He yawned, which ruined the effect. Then he turned out the light and climbed into bed. "You'll probably sleep with one eye open, and that's okay. But we both need the rest."

"Fair enough." Gage lay down and got comfortable. Forge wound his fingers into Gage's and lay still. Soon Forge's breathing evened out and he was truly asleep. After that, it didn't take long for Gage's mind to stop whirring, and he too fell to sleep.

"GOD, I slept hard," Forge said as he walked into the kitchen, dressed and ready for the day. Gage had also, at least for enough hours that he didn't feel like his ass was dragging on the ground.

"I slept well, and there were no issues, and I already worked the perimeter. Harv is on his way over and should be here any minute." Gage's phone dinged, and he saw the message from Harv. "We can go now. The house is in good hands… and eyes." He deactivated the alarms, and they left the house through the garage and got into his car. Forge opened the garage door, and Gage backed out, waited for the door to close once again, then pulled away from the house in the opposite direction than the one they intended to go. He began taking a very circuitous route into town to throw off anyone who might be trying to follow them. Once he was convinced he wasn't followed, Gage drove to the freeway and took a few unnecessary exits and on-ramps just to be sure.

The downtown building was massive, built at a time when banks created monoliths to demonstrate just how solid their foundation was. It was a show of might and power to hide the fact that they were really built on nothing more than air and whatever illusion of strength they could create.

Gage pulled into the underground lot and left it again immediately to park in the back of an open lot nearby. "It was too enclosed, and if we needed to get out, we could easily have found ourselves trapped." He led Forge to the side entrance and into the massive bank lobby.

"I always love coming here, especially at Christmas." Forge looked around at the various displays, keeping close, and Gage did his best to keep Forge behind him in case something happened, acting as a shield.

68

"Good morning, gentlemen," Detective Coleridge said as he approached.

"Morning," Forge said, and Gage did the same. "The safe-deposit boxes are downstairs." Forge indicated the set of steps, and they descended, walking back in time. The walls were paneled in dark, rich wood, and all the desks were heavy and probably from when the building was built back in the twenties. They went right over to the safe-deposit desk, and when Coleridge showed his badge, the lady behind it scurried to get a manager.

"May I help you?" asked a man in his fifties, with slightly graying hair and dressed in an impeccable gray suit. His facial expression said he clearly wasn't impressed.

Forge handed him the keys and told the manager his name, as well as provided Granger's.

"He's deceased," Coleridge added in a tone meant to intimidate.

The manager went over to a computer and typed for a moment. "Yes. I have the records, and Mr. Reynolds is listed on the box." He presented Forge with a paper to sign, then led the way into the vault. "Only the box holder is allowed inside. You can meet him in one of the private review rooms if Mr. Reynolds agrees." He turned, and Gage and Coleridge stayed outside while Forge retrieved the box, struggling slightly. Then the three of them were shown into a small conference room with a table and chairs. The manager left the room, and Forge lifted the lid on the box.

"Holy shit," he said as he took out a sleeve of gold coins, then another and a third.

"Where did those come from?" Detective Coleridge asked.

"I'm not sure." Forge placed them to the side and fixed Coleridge with a stare when he reached for them. "We'll do this my way. You may see anything that's in here, but you can take nothing that isn't specifically relevant." Forge removed three more sleeves of coins and set them aside. Then he pulled out papers and looked them over before handing them to Coleridge.

"These look like notes of some sort, but I can't read them." He showed them to Forge and Gage. "Can either of you?"

"No," Forge answered, and Gage shook his head.

"Why would he write notes in some sort of code?" Detective Coleridge leaned closer.

"They aren't. It's German," Forge said. "Granger loved languages and spoke German and Italian fluently. His parents are Italian, and it was spoken in their home. He learned German in school. It should be possible to get these translated. We can make you copies, as long as you promise to share with me what they say. Regardless of the content."

Gage smiled at Forge's take-charge attitude. He liked that Forge was keeping control of what was now his.

Under the papers were stock certificates that Forge let Coleridge see. He made notes and then handed them back. "And you didn't know about any of this?"

"Not that I can think of. Granger might have talked about some investments he was making, but he and I haven't been on deep-discussion terms in months. He could have been squirreling things away so they didn't become part of the divorce." Forge cleared his throat. "What a jackass." He gripped the edge of the table, arms shaking. "He and I did everything together for years. I helped him out when he started the firm and needed money to get it off the ground. I supported him in so many ways, and this is how he acts?" He sighed deeply. "Maybe I should have known. Granger always liked to win. No matter what, he was a lawyer and winning was everything."

Forge shook himself as though trying to physically cast off what must have been deep betrayal and hurt. Frankly, the more Gage learned about Granger, the more he was coming to dislike him. He seemed selfish. It was obvious that Granger had plenty and that Forge had been part of the reason for his wealth. Hiding things seemed too damned petty and childish.

"Is there anything else?" Coleridge asked, and Forge slowly reached inside once more to the back of the large metal container.

He removed another of those damned boxes, like the ones he had at home, only this one was smaller.

"Wow," Forge said as he carefully set it on the table. "It's jade, and from the look of it, Chinese." He inspected it and smiled a little. "It's another puzzle box, only this one is much older than the others." He lifted and jiggled it gently. "There's something inside."

"Can you open it?" Detective Coleridge asked.

Forge shook his head. "Not right now. I need to look it over and see if I can figure it out. And don't even think of breaking or forcing it. The quality of work is exquisite, and this is probably four hundred years old and worth as much as a house." He set the box down once again, checked the safe-deposit box, waited for Coleridge to make his copies, and then placed everything back inside with the exception of the puzzle box, which Forge handed to Gage to hold. It was cold to the touch, solid, heavy, and incredibly beautiful. Forge closed the box, and as they left the room, the bank manager met them to escort Forge back into the vault to put it back into its slot.

Gage wished he had something to put the jade box into to protect it. He ended up ducking into the bathroom, where he unbuttoned his shirt and removed his T-shirt to wrap the box in it, then put his shirt back on before emerging. He cradled the wrapped box in his arms to protect it as he waited for Forge, then followed him up the stairs, watching everyone around them, with Coleridge behind him. All three of them left the building together.

"You will call me if and when you open the box and let me know what's inside?"

"Of course," Forge said. "And just so you're aware, I went through the contents of the home safe again and all I found was a drive with the electronic copies of the will and other papers. I thought you'd like to know."

Detective Coleridge nodded and made some notes.

"He also opened each of the puzzle boxes in the house and found nothing," Gage offered, figuring it was best for them to be as honest and forthright as possible.

"I would like to know when I can clean up the office and put everything back together. It bothers me that there's a room in my own home that I can't enter," Forge said.

Coleridge looked up from his notes, appearing thoughtful. "I'd like to come over tomorrow, and we can go through the office again. Then you can have the room back."

That seemed to make Forge happy. "Then we'll see you tomorrow and we can talk about the box as well. I hope I can get it open. Figuring them out was Granger's expertise, but he taught me a lot." He bit his lower lip.

"We'll talk tomorrow, and I'll see about having the German document translated."

Gage was pleased to see that Coleridge seemed to be keeping up his half of the deal. Granted, Coleridge was best equipped to figure out what Granger was up to and why, as well as who had killed him. But Gage was becoming convinced that they were all going to need to work together in order to unravel this mystery.

"Thank you." Forge turned away toward the street, but stopped and went back to where Coleridge stood. "Granger loved puzzles—I told you that. But what I'm starting to think is that whatever these files are, Granger might have protected them using a puzzle of his own device."

Coleridge furrowed his brow. "I don't understand."

"Granger not only worked puzzles, but he used to love making them. When he read fiction, it was adventure novels, and he used to see if he could work out what the author was putting together for the hero to follow. He always said the good ones were those he couldn't work out."

"What makes you think he made his own puzzle?" Coleridge asked, his expression urgent, hungry.

"Gut instinct from what I know of Granger. The hard part is that we don't know what the pieces look like or if there's really a puzzle at all. But think about it—he put this puzzle box with something inside it in the safe-deposit box at the bank. He could have just as easily put it in the safe at home."

"What if he was trying to hide it from you?" Gage asked.

"That's possible. But what if he was trying to keep it and what's inside from the people who killed him?" Forge raised his eyebrows. Coleridge nodded, and Gage admitted to himself that Forge might have a point. "As soon as I get it open, I promise to call you, but it could take a while."

Coleridge rubbed at a spot above his left eye. "I'm not happy about this, but I don't think I have any other choice. I don't know anyone with any expertise in these."

Gage knew Coleridge would much rather have control of everything. "We understand," he said, tilting his head toward where he'd parked the car. "We'll definitely be in touch tomorrow, if not sooner." He handed Forge the wrapped box, guiding him to the car, got him inside, and started the engine as quickly as possible. He didn't wait for seat belts and jumped out into traffic as soon as he had an opening.

Forge held the wrapped box tightly on his lap. "I hate to ask and it isn't convenient, but I need to stop at my office to check in, and I should do the same at Granger's."

"That isn't a good idea."

"But do you want to have to come back?" Forge sounded agitated, so Gage passed by the freeway on-ramp as Forge told him the building his office was in. They made it with no incidents, and Gage was grateful for underground parking with multiple exits to different streets. Forge got out of the car, still carrying the box. "I can get a bag when we're inside and give you your T-shirt back." He grinned, leading Gage to the elevators and up to his floor.

"Forge!" the receptionist called at damn near the top of her lungs.

Forge handed the box to Gage just as every cubicle and office emptied out and surrounded him, twelve to fourteen people all talking at once, offering their support and any help he would need.

"Who's this?" a women in her early thirties asked with a sly grin. "And where have you been hiding him?"

"This is Gage. He's an old friend who's helping to keep me safe. With everything that's happened, my lawyer and I thought some extra protection might be in order."

Forge was hugged by each man and woman as they filtered back to their desks. He was cared for a great deal, and that warmed Gage's heart, knowing Forge was truly as amazing as he was coming to rediscover.

"Do you have time to go over a few things?" a young lady of about twenty-five with long, flowing mahogany hair asked. "I know this has all been really hard for you and I'm so sorry about it, but…."

"I know, Pam. The world doesn't stop just because something bad happens." Forge motioned them to an office with his name on the plaque, and they all stepped inside. Forge patiently answered a myriad of questions that went completely over Gage's head, but Forge either knew the answer, had what sounded like a solid opinion, or was able to direct her to the person she could contact. It was a thing of logistical beauty to behold. "You can call me on my cell phone if you need anything. At the moment I'm sitting tight at home for my protection."

"What about the funeral?" She closed the notebook she'd used to record Forge's answers to her questions.

"Granger's family is going to arrange it, but the police haven't released his body yet. Hopefully fairly soon, and then who knows. His parents know things were rough between the two of us and don't feel comfortable with me planning it. Honestly, I'm kind of relieved. I'll send a message to you to post in the office with all the details once I have them." Forge stepped behind his desk and pulled out a canvas tote bag in lavender. He passed it over, along with a piece of soft fabric. Probably a sample.

Gage waited for Pam to leave before rewrapping the box and placing it gently in the bag. Then he removed his shirt, put his T-shirt back on, and sat in one of Forge's chairs as he worked at his desktop computer. "What about your boss?"

"He's in Asia on a scouting trip for a client who wants to decorate her home in authentic antiques," Forge answered as he typed rapidly. "I'm sending him an email update... now... and as soon as I go through all these.... Okay. I can handle the rest from home." He stood and shut down the system.

Forge said goodbye as they left, and Gage scanned everyone, trying to appear nonthreatening even as he watched for any signs of unusual behavior.

"I don't think going to Granger's office is a good idea," Gage said once they were in the elevator.

"I understand, but he has the same kind of desk at the office as he did at home. As far as I know, he didn't use the compartment for his computer. So what else is in it? The firm is not going to allow the police anywhere near them without court orders up the wazoo, but I can get in without anyone thinking twice about it. I'll simply say I need to collect some of his personal things." He smiled, and Gage had to admit Forge had him. His curiosity was piqued.

"What do you suggest we do with the box?"

Forge made sure it was wrapped carefully in the bag and slid it under his seat. "No one will see a thing, and you can stay in the car with it if you want. I know it sounds reckless, but we need to see what's there, and no one should know that we have this."

"No. I'll carry it. Hopefully no one will think twice about it." How could a lavender bag not be conspicuous? This had to be the craziest idea, and yet he was going along with it because he wanted to make Forge happy. "Just follow my instructions and be prepared to get down or run like hell if anything happens. The bank and your office are one thing, but I wasn't expecting to spend the day running around downtown."

"I won't be very long." Forge sat back, seeming to know he'd won. Gage drove the six blocks to the high-rise that housed Granger's law firm, parked in an open lot, and they checked in with the front desk. Forge was obviously known to them because they waved him right on through, and he took the elevator to the twelfth floor. It opened into a spacious lobby that screamed "success" and "money," with an undercurrent of "we like to win."

"Good morning, Deann," Forge said as he approached the desk.

The professionally dressed lady greeted him with a half smile. "I'm sorry about your loss." She didn't sound sorry at all, but Gage kept that to himself.

"Thank you. I'm here to get a few personal things out of Granger's office. I'm sure you've already secured the sensitive materials." Forge didn't wait for an answer and led Gage right through the lushly appointed space to a corner office. It wasn't as big as he expected, but the paneled walls and massive, highly polished desk oozed money and luxury.

"Check for the hidden space," Gage said softly as he lowered himself into a chair, and Forge went to the business end of the desk and sat down.

"Forge," a man said as he breezed into the room, wearing a highly tailored suit that had to cost what Gage made in a week.

"Francis." Forge came around and received a man-hug with little warmth. "I just wanted to pick up a few of Granger's personal things."

While they were speaking, Gage placed the bag with the puzzle box on the floor on the far side of the chair, hopefully out of sight, though he kept hold of the handle.

"I understand." Francis sat in another of the high-backed visitor chairs and made himself at home before turning to Gage with a stare that must intimidate half the juries in the state. Gage stared right back. If the guy wanted a pissing contest, he'd get out his ruler. He'd met plenty of men like Francis. "And you are?"

"This is Gage. He's an old friend who's helping me through all this. There's so much to go through, and I needed some help, as well as some extra protection." Forge sat in Granger's chair while Gage wished they could get on with what they came for. But he suspected Forge didn't want to snoop while Francis was here. "This is Granger's business partner, Francis Peterborough."

"Well, as long as you're safe. That's what counts." Francis stopped glaring at Gage to turn to Forge. "In the next few weeks, you and I will need to sit down and review a buyout of Granger's share of the firm, which, with him gone, has been greatly diminished. It's sad but true."

Gage swallowed hard to keep from lashing out. What a slime! His business partner was dead and this guy was trying to stiff his estate of the fair value of one of his assets.

"Of course." Forge shifted in the chair, appearing uncomfortable.

"Why wouldn't you use a private firm to value the practice?" Gage offered, and Francis's eyes darkened to near black, though Forge nodded.

"I think that's fair." Forge sat up straighter and leaned forward on the desk. "I know according to the firm's bylaws that I can't take over Granger's ownership because I'm not a lawyer and that's what's required, but I'm also not in a hurry to settle anything. And since the fiscal year completes in six weeks, I'll see that through and will expect Granger's usual payout. Then I'll either sell his portion to another qualified attorney or you can buy me out. Either way, there isn't going to be a discount or a fire sale." Forge ran his hands over the top of Granger's desk. "This desk is fairly comfortable, so maybe I'll decide to use it."

Gage coughed slightly to cover up a chuckle. Francis looked about ready to swallow his teeth.

The surprise lasted only a few seconds, and then Francis covered it up. "No one is trying to do anything other than what's fair."

"I understand that, and decisions will be made in time without rushing. Granger always told me that decisions like this should be made with all due diligence." Forge smiled, and Francis stood, a little shakily.

"Let me know if there's anything any of us can do for you."

"I will. Thank you. Once we have the schedule, I'll send you the funeral details." Forge didn't move until Francis left, and then he motioned for Gage to close the door. As soon as the latch clicked, Forge slid back and pulled open the drawer like the one in the desk at home.

"Intentionally pissing him off?"

"Yeah. He's nosy as hell—always has been. Francis is a great lawyer, but he *has* to know everything that's going on and stick his nose in it. Granger metaphorically bloodied it more than once." Forge pulled out the contents of the drawer, and Gage opened the lavender bag. Forge slipped the papers inside and closed things up, relatching the drawer in place. "Let's get out of here. I'm tired and I want to be home."

Gage picked up the bag and opened the door, letting Forge lead the way out. Unlike Forge's office, where everyone seemed happy to see him and acted like Forge was part of their family, here it was staid. Gage kept a close lookout until they reached the elevator, which they rode back to the garage.

"Let's go quickly." Gage handed Forge the bag, paid the parking, and took off out of the garage, going as quickly as he could around the block, then taking a zigzagging route toward the freeway.

"What is it?" Forge asked. "You keep looking in the mirror."

"Lower your visor and use the mirror. See the dark blue sedan about three cars back? It got behind us two blocks after we left the office, peeled off, and it's back now." Gage made another turn, slowing down, and sure enough, the blue car did the same.

"I see it."

"Excellent. You watch them and I'm going to try to lose them. Make sure you have a good hold on something and are buckled in well." Gage shifted lanes and then, at the last minute, swerved and made a left. A car honked at him, but he didn't give a damn. The blue sedan didn't make the turn, but they were far from out of the woods. He made a quick right down an alley, then another left, continuing on. He made another turn, emerging from the alley and onto the street. He decided that rather than make for the freeway right away, it would be better to use surface streets and smaller roads that wouldn't be expected, at least for a while.

"Martin Luther King will take us north," Forge said, watching the mirror. "I don't see the car, but if they truly were following us, they're going to be looking." He looked in both directions and in the mirror as Gage drove as quickly as he dared. He didn't see anyone either, and once he reached Locust, he hurried to the freeway for the trip north.

"The stupid thing is that if we are being followed, they have to know we're most likely going to your house. Why act like this?" Gage said, then called Harv. "Anything at the house?"

"All is quiet. Why?" Harv sounded miffed through the Bluetooth connection.

"We believe we picked up a tail. So I was wondering if you've seen anything," Gage said as he picked up speed, going with traffic and doing his best not to stand out. Instinct told him to go as fast as he could, but his training overrode that. They'd lost the tail, so he needed to blend in.

"I'll call if I do—wait…. Yes, we have a car that just pulled up down the block." Harv grew quiet for a moment, then said, "They're sitting inside. I'll watch them."

"Description…?"

"Black, late-model Toyota from the look of it."

"All right. Keep me informed." Gage disconnected, his mind racing. Whoever they were up against was escalating. "We sure pissed someone off somehow."

"I guess. But where? Was it someone at the bank, my office, or Granger's office?"

"Maybe none of the above. We could have been followed all morning and I just happened to notice them now, and since we've shaken the tail, they're waiting for us at the house, not realizing that we've got that watched." Gage's mind ran in a number of directions, ticking off possibilities. "One thing is for sure. We aren't going to the house." He exited at Brown Deer Road and drove west, working his way around to his office, where he could park out of sight and they could regroup to figure out what their next move was going to be.

"The blue car behind us is getting…." Forge yelped as it banged into them. The rear of their car skidded, and Gage pressed the accelerator to the floor, flying down the wide street. He made a turn and then another, trying to shake them. "Jesus!"

"Hold on." Gage braked and turned, the rear end fishtailing, but the front-wheel drive pulled them out and the car leaped forward. The black car behind them didn't make the turn, and Gage watched for a second as the car went up on its side and continued rolling, over and over, before coming to rest in the parking lot of an empty bank building. Gage didn't stick around to see if the driver was okay. "Call Coleridge and let him know what's going on and that he needs to get people out to the accident. Hopefully they aren't injured enough to keep them from talking." He sped up once again and drove the rest of the way to the office. Using his remote to open the door, he pulled right inside and closed it behind them. They jumped out of the car and rode the elevator up to his floor.

"Margie," he called. "Make sure we aren't being followed." He continued through to his office.

"I don't see anything," she said as he passed her desk. "I take it you had a little problem?"

"Yes. We'll be staying here for a while."

"The kitchen area is stocked with the basics, and you know we're alarmed more than Fort Knox. What happened?"

"Apparently we've stirred up a hornet's nest and we have no idea why. Persons unknown think we have something they want, and dammit all if we know who they are or even what they're looking for." It was so frustrating. He turned to Forge, who was standing right behind him. He led him through to the temporary living quarters. "Are you okay? Did you get banged up?" Gage sure as hell hoped not. "Sometimes when I get into evasive mode—"

"I'm okay, and you were amazing." Forge beamed at him. "You knew exactly what to do, and when that car hit us, you…."

He kicked the door closed, set the bag on the floor, and kissed Gage with enough heat to set the place on fire.

Gage forgot about boxes and papers, as well as puzzles and damn near anything else, as he wound his arms around Forge and returned the kiss that had both of them shaking. Gage wasn't sure if it was the postchase high, but he wasn't going to question it. He devoured Forge's lips as he tugged at his shirt, getting it off and dropped to the floor so he could have access to all that luscious skin.

"You make me safe," Forge groaned when their lips parted.

"As long as you're okay." Gage kissed Forge again just as his phone rang. He pulled away with a deep growl and yanked the phone out of his pocket.

"They're still waiting," Harv said. "What do you want me to do?"

"Scare the ever-loving shit out of them. The bastards here rear-ended me and tried to kill both of us. How you do it is fully up to you." Gage chuckled. "And have fun."

Harv signed off, and Gage smiled as he put his phone back in his pocket.

"I take it they're still at the house."

"Harv will take care of it."

Forge nodded. "So I heard." He seemed amused as he picked up his shirt to pull it back on. The moment seemed to have passed… at least for now. Once he was fully dressed again, Forge picked up the bag and carried it to the sofa, sat down, and took out the papers. He set them in a neat pile before removing the box and placing it on the table. "This really is exquisite. The light color is the most desirable, and the quality of the carving is mind-blowing. You expect the dragons to begin to move at any second."

"What will you do?" Gage asked, sitting next to him.

"We need to identify the various pieces of stone, and then we might be able to see how they'll move." Forge turned the box around in his hands, but Gage couldn't see where there were any pieces. It looked solid, and yet there was definitely something inside. "See, this is one piece, right here, and this is another."

"How can you tell?"

"They made the joins in the stone part of the design, but these lines are a little more defined than some of the others. What I need to find is the initial piece. None of those will move. So I have to find the lock, the one part that starts everything." Forge moved his fingers over the various parts of the dragon design, carefully studying it. "I'm not seeing anything more." He set the box back on the table and picked up the papers. He glanced at them and handed some to Gage. "Take a look. Even I know who these people are."

Gage took the pages and skimmed through them. "Holy crap! How did he get involved with these people? They break legs for looking at them the wrong way." Gage read through each of the papers, which were contracts and details of various bank accounts.

"Yeah." Forge looked over the rest of the pages and handed them to him. "I think we know who's after us… at least who might be after us. But—" Forge stopped, the page he was holding fluttering as his hand shook. "You need to see this."

Gage took the page, read it over, and it wasn't until he took a second look that he noticed the name at the top of the document. Harrison Livingston, his father. It couldn't be, and yet the document contained his father's name and address, as well as the same phone number he currently had in his phone directory. The document also listed financial transfers, dates, and amounts, as well as vague reasons for the money. "What the hell?"

"Bribes and payoffs that the Lucci family was making. I'm willing to bet these are only some of what Granger had, and he was keeping them in the desk as a kind of insurance."

"But to my parents?" Gage swore under his breath.

"Well, to your dad…." Forge let the thought hang.

"My mother and father are like half of one person. If he did anything without her, she'd have his nuts for lunch. And my mother is just as dependent on my dad. They're like a well-oiled machine.

So if this is true, then my holier-than-thou parents—the ones who don't understand me being gay and the ones who most likely intercepted your letter all those years ago—are up to their ears in some pretty shady shit." He kept looking at the page, hoping like hell it wasn't true. Even in the back of his mind, he wondered if this could be something fake. Maybe it was designed to blackmail his parents or something, though why would Granger hide a fake document in a secret compartment in his desk? In case someone stumbled on it? That didn't seem likely.

"This is turning out to be a huge mess." Forge continued scanning each document and handing them to Gage, who reviewed each one and set them aside. Some of the documents lacked context, and neither of them knew what they meant, but Gage looked them over, filing away the information for later reference. "What do we do with all this?"

Gage breathed as evenly as possible. They were sitting on a potential powder keg. "Let me think. If we go public with this…."

"My gut is telling me to hold on to them. If Granger kept them as insurance, then we're going to need some too… and more. After all, Granger's dead."

"Okay." Gage stood, pacing the floor. "What do we do with it?"

"When we get back to the house, hide it in Granger's desk? They didn't find it when they looked before, so they aren't going to find it now. If something were to happen to me, Detective Coleridge knows about the desk drawer, and maybe we can make sure he would get notified."

"That's possible. We can certainly set up a nuclear bomb type thing. I've done it many times in the past. Mostly I work with wives needing protection on their husbands, and they tend to know things the men don't want made public. I set up an automatic information release if a set of circumstances are met. The second piece is a little trickier in our case. With a divorce we simply make sure the other party knows to behave and is aware of the consequences. That's harder in this case." Gage scratched his head and stacked the papers together, retrieving an envelope from his office and sliding the papers inside. "Let's think this through before we decide on anything. Maybe the contents of the box will help us figure out what we want to do or can help the police."

"But I can't get it open," Forge said.

"You will. I have faith in you." Gage smiled and sat back down, putting his arm around Forge's shoulders. "Just give your mind a chance to work on it." The high-powered energy from earlier had dissipated, and though Gage missed it, sitting quietly next to Forge was pleasant and surprisingly satisfying. Gage was an action guy, had been most of his life, so being quiet with someone was a relatively new experience for him, at least as part of his recent experience.

"Gage," Forge whispered, leaning against the arm of the sofa.

"Yeah…?"

"You aren't going to disappear in a puff of smoke or something, are you?" Forge sounded like a small child at that moment, asking about his worst fear.

"Why would I?" He'd gotten the one thing he'd always wanted and dreamed of, a chance to reengage with Forge.

Forge turned to him, sitting upright. "I thought Granger would be with me forever. We had promised to be there and live our lives together. Then he decided I wasn't good enough and stepped out with some twink. The grass was greener somewhere else. And to make it worse, Granger didn't even care about the guy. He just messed up everything we had for nothing."

"You know none of that was your fault." Gage could almost see the hurt gathering around Forge like a deep shadow growing darker around him. "You didn't deserve to be cheated on, and you didn't do anything to make Granger want to leave. Whatever happened, and whatever he did, was his issue."

"But I wasn't enough for him. I should have known what he wanted and been able to keep him happy." Forge frowned.

Gage groaned softly. "I see this with my clients all the time. You can never be responsible for someone else's happiness. Most people don't understand that happiness is internal. It's like a spring from within, and if Granger's spring ran dry and he thought he needed to look somewhere else, other than you, then that was his problem. Yes, other people can make us unhappy, but our happiness or ultimate lack of it is our own. We own it."

Forge turned and leaned a little closer. "But he said I wasn't what he needed anymore."

"He decided that, and he was the one who walked away from the relationship. But he did it for his own reasons, and contrary to what he wanted you to believe, it was his decision, his fault, and he owns it. Even though he's dead, Granger doesn't get a pass unless you give him one." Gage shifted closer, and Forge leaned against him. Gage pulled Forge a little closer. He had no idea if Forge understood what he was trying to say, but it had to be said.

"What are you going to do about your family?" Forge asked.

"I don't know." Here he was giving Forge advice about happiness when a piece of his own potential happiness had been chipped away by those documents. "But whatever happens, I'm not the one to blame." Still, when something happened that was good in his life, something else went to hell.

CHAPTER 5

FORGE WONDERED why in the hell he'd opened up like that. For eight months he'd stewed and wondered what he'd done wrong.

"My mother abandoned me," Forge said out of the blue. His mouth seemed to have developed a case of verbal diarrhea, and he couldn't control the path between his brain and mouth.

Gage grew sad. "I know that. You and I spent all that time alone, talking to each other. Your mother had a lot of nervous issues and had difficulties coping, so your dad raised you. I know that your favorite color is green and that you blamed yourself for her going away, just like you blame yourself for Granger's cheating. I know that you love strawberry ice cream but don't eat it because you didn't want the guys to see you eating pink food. I bet you still look at it longingly in the store and pass it by." Gage pulled him closer, and the vulnerability that had engulfed him lessened.

"There's a lot about me you don't know," Forge challenged. A hell of a lot had changed in the seventeen years they'd been apart. "And I bought strawberry ice cream… once." He held Gage a little tighter. "Granger hated it and asked why I bought the pink shit."

Gage shook his head. "You can get any kind of ice cream you want." He tilted Forge's head up until his gaze bored into him. "When you were with me for that night, you slept on the right side of the bed, but I noticed that your things were on the left upstairs. I'm willing to bet that was what Granger preferred and you went along with it."

"Damn." Forge needed to remember that old eagle eyes here saw everything.

"I know you're the kindest, most un-self-serving man I've ever met, and Granger made you think you needed him, when I bet he was the one who needed you." Gage leaned closer to touch his lips to Forge's. "What makes me angry is that Granger took the man I loved, the one I fell in love with all those years ago, and made him doubt himself. And the bastard did that to cover up his own doubts and fears. I'm guessing he had to be the best at whatever he did, and that meant you had to come in second... all the damn time."

As much as Forge wanted to argue with Gage, he couldn't. He and Granger had been happy, but Gage was right. They'd been happy as long as Forge was willing to support Granger's career and aspirations. Once Forge's career took off and he had a larger clientele, Granger had become needy and desperate for as much attention as possible. "How do you know all this?"

"I watch you and I see you for who you are. I bet Granger never did."

Forge closed his eyes, considering if what Gage had said was true. Sure, he'd loved Granger, and they had spent many years together, but now he wondered if maybe he'd only been convenient. Granger had said that he'd only cheated the one time, but what if that wasn't true? "Granger was the master of his own reality. I think that's what made him a good lawyer."

Gage hummed his agreement. "What did you fall in love with? What was it about Granger that attracted you in the first place?"

Forge stilled for a few seconds. "Back then, Granger was driven and ready to take on the world." He lifted his gaze, tilting his head to the side. "You should have seen him. I think in some ways, at least then, he was a lot like you. He made his career by taking on one of the huge automobile companies because they didn't want to take financial responsibility for faulty door latches. They kept trying to pass it off on the supplier even though they knew the latches they were receiving were bad. They installed them anyway. Granger worked night and day for months, not even knowing if he was ever going to see a dime out of it. But he said it was the right thing to do." Forge groaned slightly when he heard the admiration that crept into his voice. For a second he hoped Gage didn't, but he *had* admired and been blown away by Granger, at least the Granger he'd been then.

"I think I remember that case. It was all over the news at the time. I thought it was impressive." Gage squeezed him a little nearer. "What happened to that Granger?"

Forge huffed. "I don't really know. I was just wondering that myself. That was the man I fell in love with. The one who put himself and everything he was on the line to help someone else. His clients had nothing at all. There was no way they could pay him up front, but when the latch failed, they lost their daughter because of it. After that…." He shrugged. "I don't know…. He seemed to chase the money, I guess. He was well-known and a lot of people clamored for him, and I thought things were good…. Maybe I was completely oblivious to how he had changed…."

"I don't think so. It's more likely Granger changed gradually." Gage really seemed to understand.

"And now I know he was keeping a lot of things from me." He and Granger had been fighting for months, but now that he really thought about it, their relationship had been over a long time before the actual breakup. "Granger used to talk to me about his cases. Not details or anything, but we used to talk and laugh about things. I used to tell him some of the weird requests I'd get from people. Like the high-profile doctor who'd seen a piece in a museum and decided he liked it so much, I was to try to find a desk just like it. The thing was, the desk was a museum piece, one of a kind, and he didn't want a reproduction. I had to explain to him that they weren't available. There was only one." Forge smiled as he shook his head. "Or the guy who wanted a Chihuly light fixture, but didn't want to pay the many thousands of dollars, so I was supposed to find someone who would make one for him. Granger and I used to laugh together over things like that." He paused as his thoughts wandered. "I think I loved the man I could laugh with and play silly word games and make up bad puns with. But I hadn't seen that man in years."

A knock on the door caused Forge to jump. Gage stood and went to open it, looking back before stepping out of the room. Forge sat back, his mind racing over what he'd said and how amazingly comfortable he felt with Gage, like the years that had separated them had suddenly disappeared. What a waste all that time had been.

"Forge," Gage said softly. "We have company." He motioned to him, and Forge went over to a bank of monitors at Margie's desk. Gage pointed to one. A dark car approached the building, circled it, and then pulled to a stop.

"I'd say you picked up some sort of electronic tail," Margie said.

Gage groaned. "I should have figured that out a while ago."

A phone rang, and Margie answered it before handing the receiver to Gage. He listened and smiled, then handed it back.

"The car outside your house is gone."

"What did Harv do?" Forge asked.

"He didn't say specifically. But the men inside were surprised when they discovered four flat tires and a wrecker showing up to tow them away. The beauty of it is that they never saw Harv at all." Gage turned to Margie, who was already back at work.

"What do you want to do about our guests?" Margie asked.

Gage turned to him, and Forge stared for a few moments.

Forge wrung his hands nervously. "Gage, can you find the tracking device?"

"I'll see. What do you have in mind?"

"You have a back door, right? And is there a way to shield the signal?"

"Yes." The edges of Gage's lips curled upward. "I like the way you think. Let me see if I can find our unwanted passenger."

"Then sneak out the back and throw it in the bed of a passing truck or something. Let's lead the bastards on a wild goose chase."

Margie slid the other desk chair over to him. "You sit here with me while he does his thing." She smiled, and Forge thanked her, chuckling, as Gage left the office area. "Okay," she said, never taking her gaze from the monitors. "What's going on with you two?"

"Is this an inquisition?" Forge teased.

"You better believe it." She wasn't threatening, but very serious. "Is this some client-protector thing for you?"

"Not for me. I knew him when we were in the service, and we reconnected a few days ago." He most certainly wasn't going to tell her how he was feeling when he wasn't totally sure himself, and if he was going to make some grand emotional declaration, Gage deserved to be the first to hear it.

"I see, and now your husband is dead and you're looking to replace him."

Forge wasn't sure how to take that, then figured what the hell. "Please. I already had one of those, and he turned out to be a lying, cheating, secret-keeping pain in the ass. So if I was looking to replace him, I'd put an ad in Manhunt. I figure I could get a clone of Granger in about three minutes."

She turned to him, her mouth a thin line for two seconds, and then she smiled. "Damn, I like you. He needs someone with a quick wit who'll challenge him and not put up with any of his crap."

"I've put up with enough shit the last eight months, I think I'm a fucking expert at shoveling the stuff. I think I can handle him." Actually, he was looking forward to it.

"Gage is a good man. Better than the first one I married. Hell, if he were older and I were younger… and he liked girls, I'd snap up that boy in a heartbeat. He's one amazing man, despite everything his family put him through." She pointed to one of the monitors, and sure enough Gage closed the door to the back of the building and ran for the shrubbery that lined the property. Margie pulled on a set of headphones. "Our visitors are still out front, probably still scratching their asses… wait, they seem to realize the sensor is on the move and are pulling around the side of the building. Now they're turning around and heading out the alley toward the road... perfect. They've stopped."

Gage emerged from the trees as a truck approached. He made a beautiful throw, and Forge wished he were close enough to have seen the actual arc, but Margie directed his attention to another monitor as the car drew to the end of the drive and made the turn to follow the old red pickup truck.

It was a thing of beauty.

"Yes, I agree. They'll probably be back when they catch up to the truck and realize they've been had," Margie said as Gage jogged to the back door and disappeared from the monitor. Forge turned as Gage joined them once again. Margie took off the headphones and set them on the desk. "What do you want me to do?"

"We're going to go to a hotel," he told her. "Go on home and work remotely. It isn't safe to be here right now. If anything happens, call the police, and they'll take off fast. The police are the last people they want to speak with." Gage turned to him, the heat in his eyes intensifying, tempered with worry. "Bring the box. We'll leave the papers here as insurance."

"I'll arrange to get your car repaired," Margie said as Forge hurried off to retrieve the box and pack it into the bag once more.

When he returned, Gage was waiting for him. Margie had already left, and Gage was watching the monitors. "All right. Let's go." He guided Forge toward the back of the building, where another car waited. This one, a Mustang, fast and powerful, sat in a gleaming garage. "Before I was trying to be inconspicuous, but now we need raw power." Gage opened the door, and Forge hurried to the passenger side. He buckled in and held the box in his arms. Gage raised the door and took off, closing it behind and using a back drive to exit the property.

"Where do you think we should go?"

"I was thinking Chicago. It's a bigger city and a lot easier to hide out. Also, since my family is somehow involved in this mess, I might need to get a message to them to back off." He turned onto

Brown Deer, traveling toward the freeway. They didn't talk much, and Forge sank into his thoughts. It wasn't until they crossed the state line that Forge felt like speaking.

"Your mom and dad…."

"Yeah. They've caused a great deal of trouble." Gage's tone suggested that was something they did quite often.

"What happened between you? I remember their letters. Your mom always wrote so caringly, wishing she could have been there with you. And the letters you sent in return were so loving as well. It was part of what I fell in love with. You were such a big guy, and even still in a bed, you exuded strength. So to be so loving to her…."

Gage sighed. "What came between us was you. I told my parents all about the hospital and how you helped me and looked after me. Maybe I talked to them too much at first, I don't know. Of course, when I didn't hear from you, I talked about you less and less."

"Way to pile on the guilt." Forge meant the comment sarcastically, but it probably didn't come out as clearly as he wanted.

Gage grimaced. "Except now we both know that you did write and my mom probably intercepted your letters. One was open, so I bet she read it, realized what was going on, and took matters into her own hands to try to put an end to it because it didn't meet her idea of how her son should behave."

"Things went bad because they found out you were gay?" Forge asked. That was so typical of people sometimes.

"Maybe that's how it started. But after I got out of the hospital, was medically discharged, and came home, Mom and Dad wanted me to go into the family trucking business. I had no interest. Can you imagine working for them all the damn time? I needed to be on my own and have my own life, and they couldn't understand that at all." Gage gripped the steering wheel hard as he continued driving. "I started my protection services company in Chicago originally, but quickly relocated it to Milwaukee because I needed to be independent."

Forge turned so he could see Gage better. "None of that sounds bad. Your parents should have been proud of you for wanting to be your own person."

"You'd think so. My parents hated that I enlisted in the Army. They thought I should have driven a truck for a while and learned the family business. Dad started it when he was in his twenties, borrowing money to buy his first truck. After that, he bought another and hired his best friend as a driver. In five years he had twelve drivers, and after another five years, he was well on his way. Now the company is national and you see his trucks everywhere. I know he wanted me to be part of that, but I wasn't interested. He pushed, but I pushed back. Then he gave me an ultimatum that I either joined him in working for the company or he'd cut me off. And I went out on my own. That was what my dad couldn't forgive."

Forge blinked and tried to get his head around what Gage was telling him. "I don't understand why that's a bad thing."

"Because I'd rather do without anything from my parents than work for my dad. I was willing to be broke and alone rather than work for him. My dad can forgive many things, but being disrespected like that, at least in his mind, was too much. After a while, when I started to make a success of the business, things thawed between us, but when I told my mother I was dating... a guy... the walls went right back up. Now we rarely talk, and when we do, it's like she and my dad are talking to one of the members of their country club that they tolerate but don't really like."

"That's so stupid. What kind of parents are they? Families are supposed to help their kids be independent, not make them stay under their thumb for the rest of their lives." Forge turned, watching out the window. There had to be more to it than that.

"My dad told me that he'd built the company so we could have a better life. He'd hoped that I'd take over and run it after he retired. I think when I turned down the job, he equated it to turning my back on him. That wasn't what I meant at all, but I think it's how he took it." Gage slowed down as they encountered a pocket of heavier traffic. "It took me a long time to figure things out, but I think it comes down to this. My dad built his business and is very successful. He made his dream come true. But the problem is that his dream also included the fact that I would take over for him. And—" Gage screwed his face up slightly as if he were trying to choose the right words. "—while it's okay to dream for yourself, it isn't okay to foist your dream off on someone else. My dad can dream all he wants for himself, but he doesn't get to decide what my dreams are. He doesn't get that, and I don't think he ever will. He's used to getting what he wants." Gage seemed relieved to get the words out. He sat straighter in the seat, and his lips and the wrinkles around his eyes smoothed away.

"Do you regret your decision?" Forge asked.

"I think sometimes I do, but most of the time, no. I think I realized a long time ago that if they weren't going to accept something as basic as me wanting to be myself and make my own way, life with them was never going to make me happy." Gage reached over, took Forge's hand, and squeezed it gently. "Things were messed up for a while, but I have good people in my life now, like Harv and Margie, as well as the rest of the men and women who work for me. Most of them I was in the service with. They acted like my family… until you came barreling back into my life."

Forge wondered how he should take that. He hoped that was a good thing. When Gage turned and smiled, outshining the sun that poured in through the windows, Forge's doubt evaporated in an instant. It wasn't just a good thing. Maybe it was the best thing.

"So where are we going now?"

"We'll find a hotel downtown and hole up there for a few days."

Forge groaned. "I can't keep my life on hold like this. I have a job. Up till now I've…." What the hell was he going to do? "I suppose I can say I need a few days' vacation time."

"Call them and arrange it. We're going to have to figure all this out pretty quickly." Gage patted the bag that contained the box. "I think the only way you can possibly be safe is to put an end to whatever is going on. If Granger was involved in something criminal, then bringing the whole thing down is what we need to do."

"Gage, we don't know shit about what's going on. Not really. We have a few papers that lead us to some criminal elements, a few pieces of what might be one of Granger's puzzles, and little else. I know we need to open this box and see what's inside, but I keep wondering, what if there's nothing? What if he put the box there for safekeeping because of how valuable it is and nothing more?"

"Granger was killed for a reason, and you aren't going to be safe until we find out what that reason is and then find a way to keep you safe. I know this isn't something you signed up for, but it's what has to be done." Gage took the 94 split toward Chicago. Traffic was heavy but moved steadily, and once they reached the downtown area, Gage exited the freeway and pulled into one of the hotels that lined the northern section of Grant Park.

Forge looked down at what he was wearing. "You do realize we don't have any luggage or clothes."

But that didn't seem to bother Gage. They went inside, and he checked them into an art nouveau masterpiece of a hotel. Once they were in their room, which was small but elegant and extremely comfortable, Gage ordered room service. When the food arrived, he charged it to the room.

Forge and Gage dug in, not speaking as they ate. Forge hadn't thought about eating with all the running and evading they'd been doing, but now that he was settled, at least for a while, his appetite caught up with him, and he ate the entire steak Gage had ordered for him.

"What do we do now?"

"Get some rest while we can. If you aren't sleepy, take another look at that box. We need to get some answers, and the ones we're looking for have to be with Granger." Gage sat on the edge of the bed and lay back, staring at the ceiling, his shirt riding up just enough to display a line of tanned skin above his jeans. When Gage raised his hands, putting them behind his head, his shirt rode up farther, and Forge's throat went dry. He reached for his water and downed what was left in the glass before setting it on the tray.

Gage lifted his head, watching him, and Forge knew he was being taunted. "You know I should try to make progress on this box." He took it out of the bag and set it gently on the table. Then he turned back to Gage, seconds from saying to hell with it. His heart already raced a little faster because of the taste of the buffet that was Gage on display. Regardless, he turned his attention back to the box, looking over the carving very carefully. There had to be a piece that either pushed inward or slid out in order to allow the first piece to move. That was how these objects worked.

Of course, his attention was most definitely elsewhere, especially as Gage sighed and his belly contracted and then relaxed.

"You're doing that on purpose." Forge turned away and went back to the jade box, his attention drawn to the heads of the dragons that wrapped around it. They fascinated him. If he were to craft a box like this, the heads of the dragons would figure into his opening mechanism somehow, but he wasn't seeing anything, which drove him crazy. He set the box aside and sat on the bed next to Gage.

"Doing what?" Gage asked innocently, and Forge lightly smacked his arm.

"Being distracting and beautiful." He ran his finger lightly over Gage's exposed belly. "You know, if you want something, all you need to do is ask." He continued stroking, sliding his finger upward and around Gage's belly button. Gage groaned and Forge stopped. "Is something bothering you?" He waggled his eyebrows. "Are you growing uncomfortable?" He eyed the bulge in Gage's pants.

"Now who's doing things on purpose?" Gage pulled his hands from under his head, and Forge leaned away. "Tease."

"I am not. You're the one who was teasing when I was trying to concentrate on the box so we could find out what was inside.

But was someone else helpful?" Forge shook his head. "No. He lay here all sexy, and I couldn't figure anything out. So I gave up to get closer to his sexiness, and he just lies there."

"Oh, he does?" Gage growled and pounced. Forge laughed as Gage tumbled him back onto the bed, hovering over him. "What else does this living embodiment of sexy do?"

"Now you're just being silly," Forge teased, and Gage growled once again, then kissed him. Forge didn't have the brain action to stop him. Not that he'd ever have wanted to.

Gage's phone rang, and he pulled away.

"I swear, one of these days I'm going to toss your pants alarm right out that damn window."

"It's Harv," Gage told him, and instantly the tension that had been with Forge since Granger's death, but had been forgotten about for a little while with Gage, came roaring right back. "What's happening? ... No, we aren't coming back. ... Not unless you really need to know." Gage began pacing slightly. "Just protect the house and scare the crap out of anyone who approaches. We're still trying to figure this whole thing out, but it's clear Granger was mixed up with some pretty bad people and they have enough money to throw a lot of people at the problem."

Forge went to the bathroom and shut the door. He sat on the closed lid of the toilet, his elbows on his knees, resting his head on his hands. This was getting to be too damned much. None of this was his fault. He hadn't gotten involved with folks who killed people. Forge sat up straight, clenching his fists. He wanted to punch the shit out of Granger. "Dang it, I wish I could bring you back just so I could smack the living hell out of you. What the fuck were you thinking?"

A soft knock sounded, and Forge told Gage to come in. "Harv says a few people have come by the house, but other than that, it's been quiet."

"Is he going to stay?"

"If you want him to," Gage answered.

"I don't want anything to happen to the house, though once this is over, I'm going to put it on the market. I need to move away from that life and build one of my own. I don't want to go back to the way I was with Granger." It was so clear now. He'd become stuck in the life he and Granger had built, and for months he'd been trying to hold on to it rather than letting go and starting over.

"That's a good sign."

"I know. Change is scary, and I've been too afraid of it to get off my ass and just start over. I think we both might have been, and maybe that was why we were fighting over every little thing." Forge stood and walked back over to the box to pick it up once again. He actually thought of smashing it just so he could get at whatever was inside. Hell, he'd break half of what he owned just to be able to have this over with, know who killed Granger, and have the chips fall where they may, just so he could have the chance to rebuild his life once more. Forge paused with his hands on the cool stone, turning to Gage and hoping like hell that the chances he was being given would include the biggest second chance of all.

Gage looked back at him, but his eyes were clouded and elsewhere. "I think I need to talk to my dad." He shivered. "Into the lion's den, so to speak. He was mentioned in those papers and has to have some answers. Then we need to contact Coleridge."

"Jesus." The thought of going near Gage's family nearly terrified him. He imagined it as some sort of gathering out of *The Godfather* or *Goodfellas*. "If you think that's what you need to do." He stepped away from the table, his heart beating faster even as he lay down on the bed and tried not to think about what Gage was planning.

"Us," Gage corrected. "I'm not leaving you."

"You want me to go with you to see your parents? It isn't like they're going to be welcoming to you or me. Do you really think they're going to tell you what we need to know if I'm there?"

Gage's devious smile should have been a clue. "I'm hoping it will throw them off enough that they'll give me whatever I want just to make themselves more comfortable." He grabbed the phone, and after a few seconds, it became apparent that Gage was calling his mother. Gage put a finger to his lips, then indicated that the speaker option was on. "Mom, I'm in Chicago and was wondering if I could see you."

"That would be lovely. Come by in the morning, and we can have breakfast. The sunroom is perfect this time of year." Dishes clinked softly in the background, telling Forge that she was most likely having tea or whatever people did in the late afternoon.

"That would be nice. But I have to return home first thing in the morning. I was hoping I could see you this evening." A more pronounced clink rang through the phone's speaker.

"Your father and I are having a party this evening, and…. Well, I suppose you could come. The people aren't your crowd, but it would be nice to see you for a few minutes." Nervousness and longing mixed in her voice. She wanted to see Gage—that was apparent. "It's a casual evening."

Gage rolled his eyes. "We'll see you about eight."

"We?" She sounded half-frightened.

"Yes, Mom. I have someone I'd like you to meet." Gage kept a smile on his lips that translated to his voice.

"I'm looking forward to it." From her tone it sounded like she half expected a herd of elephants to arrive at her door.

Gage ended the call and shoved his phone in his pocket. Forge hoped he'd join him on the bed, but Gage began pulling on the shoes he'd taken off earlier.

"We need to go shopping."

"She said it was casual."

"Which is my mother's code for dressed to the nines, but not wearing tuxedos. We'll go shopping, get what we need, and then we can come back here and clean up." Gage stepped closer. "I thought we might conserve water and shower together."

Now that was something Forge could agree to.

TWO HOURS of shopping and a quick dinner later, they arrived back at the hotel. Gage made double sure they weren't followed. "We have an hour before we need to leave." Gage dropped the bags on the bed and pulled Forge into his arms. "Come on. Let's get cleaned up, and I'll do my best to wipe the nervous curve off your lips."

"You know your mom and dad aren't going to go out of their way to make me feel comfortable." Forge shifted from foot to foot.

"This isn't about them making you welcome. I don't really care what they think about you." Gage held him tighter. "Their opinion about most things in my life ceased to matter some time ago. Remember, we're there to find out some of my father's business contacts and to ultimately get him to spill the beans on who he's been dealing with and what he was being paid off to do. The reason you're there is to keep both of them off-balance."

Forge wrinkled his brow. "I don't understand."

"You will. Trust me. My mother is going to hover near us most of the night because she's going to be worried I'll say something to someone that will embarrass her. The only time she won't do that is when I'm talking to my father, and he'll want to do that alone if he can manage it. See, my dad will make another pitch to get me to work for him—he always does. When that happens, I should be able to steer things the way I want them."

"How?" Forge still didn't get how this was going to work.

"I'm going to use my dad's hopes against him. I told you his dream. Well, he never gives up, and I'll have to dangle some bait in front of him if I'm ever going to get him to open up." Gage turned away and toed off his shoes, then pulled off his shirt. Usually the sight of Gage's back, and then his chest as he turned around, was enough to make Forge forget just about anything, but in those few moments, he recognized a piece of Granger in Gage, and he shivered as a chill ran over his skin. Gage's eyes were hard and cold, but within a few seconds, they'd warmed and heated as he slowly stepped closer to where Forge stood.

"Is this really necessary?" Forge asked. He hated the thought of what he'd seen for those few seconds. "You're relishing this, and while I agree that your dad doesn't have the right to foist his dreams on you, is this the man you really are?"

Gage shook his head slowly. "This isn't about revenge. I don't have any reason to be angry with them. They are who they are, and I can't change them. I have my own life. But we need answers from them, and I know one way to get it. Dad isn't going to easily admit that he's taking bribes, who from, or why." Gage stroked his cheek. "Think of it this way. If my father is taking bribes, as the document Granger had shows, then he's part of the problem. We can either do nothing and keep running and hiding, or go after the beast itself."

Forge took a deep breath and nodded. It was time to do something. "I'm tired of running. I've had enough of feeling like a scared rabbit."

Gage didn't say anything more. He simply reached for the hem of Forge's shirt and tugged it up over his head. Forge raised his arms, and when the fabric fell to the floor, Gage pulled them together. Chest to chest, he stroked Forge's cheek, caressing him with such sweet caring. Forge closed his eyes and drank in the gentleness. He hated to admit it, but he needed to be needed and wanted, and it was even better to be cared for.

Gage cupped his jaw and slowly slid his hand around to the back of Forge's head, cradling it, then brought their lips together in a kiss that left Forge weak in the knees. Instantly the coldness he'd seen was forgotten as a bubble of heat surrounded him. His heart pulsing, blood singing in his ears, Forge gave himself to Gage, needing what he had to offer as desperately as a man lost in the desert craved water. Forge parted his lips, and Gage deepened the kiss, holding him still, dominating his mouth, pouring as much energy and passion into it as Forge had ever known in his life. Gage tugged open Forge's pants, and they fell to the floor, pooling around his legs. He stepped out of them, and Gage pressed him back. "Should we take this to the bathroom?"

"God, yes," Forge answered with a quiver of excitement as Gage ran a finger over his right nipple, sending a spark of desire shooting through him.

Gage released him, took his hand to lead him to the bathroom, and closed the door behind them. Forge stripped off the last of his clothes, watching as Gage did the same, the remainder of his amazing body coming into full view.

For an instant an image of Gage in the hospital flashed in his mind. He'd been strong then, but his legs were nothing like the wide, powerful appendages they were now. Gage had changed a lot. Even in his hospital bed, he'd had an air of strength, but now, in his prime, no one would ever guess that at one time Gage had been largely helpless and that he'd allowed Forge to see him like that and even help care for him.

"Where are you?" Gage asked softly.

There was no use lying. "Back in the hospital, years ago."

"For God's sake, why?" Gage kicked off the last of his clothes, standing with his legs spread slightly apart, cock jutting out strong and thick. "I'm nothing like that now."

"Physically, you aren't, but you're still that person." Forge closed the gap between them. "I know you don't want to remember how things were back then, but I do. You were special."

"No. You were the one who was special. Not me. You sat with me and spent all your time there when you could have been doing something much more interesting than sitting beside my bed, reading to me and writing my letters." Gage rested his head on Forge's shoulder. "I've never told a single living soul this, but you're the reason I am who I am."

Forge blinked. "Why?"

"After I was shipped home and you were relocated, I decided I needed to get better, get strong again, for you."

Forge clutched Gage tighter. He knew what was coming next; he could feel it deep in his bones. "You got strong for me and then you never got my letters."

"Yeah. I nearly gave up, but I couldn't by then. I was walking and I had a goal. If you didn't want me, then I'd learn to walk and be strong so someone else would." Gage scoffed. "Little did I know that there was no one else who could take your place. God knows I tried."

"Tell me you didn't spend seventeen years as a monk." Forge reached between them to curl his fingers around Gage's cock. "Wait, you told me you had boyfriends and things."

"Yeah, I did, and I compared them all to you. None of them was good enough." Gage groaned softly when Forge gripped him tighter, stroking slowly. "See, you already had my heart, and no one else was strong enough to manage to sway it."

Forge reached into the shower and turned on the water. He didn't want to move away, and somehow, with some laughter and even a near miss where they both almost tumbled to the floor in a fit of giggles and grabby hands, they made it into the shower. It was delightful, and once the hot water hit his skin, it seemed to ramp up the electricity between them. Forge pressed Gage against the back tile of the shower, angling the water so it ran down his chest, then slid to his knees. Gage quivered in front of him, cock bobbing up and down in anticipatory excitement. Forge leaned forward and let the head slip between his lips, then sank them slowly down the shaft.

"Forge," Gage croaked, pressed back against the tile. "Don't stop. Please, for the love of God, don't stop."

Forge had no intention of doing so, and bobbed his head hard, sucking deeply, pulling at Gage's cock with each upward movement. Gage's leg shook, and Forge pushed him back against the tile, holding Gage still as he did his level best to send Gage flying.

"Forge…," he groaned. "Not…."

Forge knew Gage meant it as a warning, but he doubled his efforts, sucking even harder until bitter saltiness flooded his mouth and Gage stilled. Forge closed his eyes, savoring Gage's flavor on his tongue before sliding back and letting the water rush over him.

Gage didn't move. He remained plastered to the tile and held still.

"Are you okay?"

Gage nodded slowly. "Oh God. Am I still alive? My head didn't explode, did it?"

Forge stood and pressed against him, his cock sliding along Gage's hip. "No. I think you're just a little overstimulated." Damn, to think he'd reduced Gage to silence. That was amazingly sexy.

"Give me a minute and I'll…," Gage murmured as Forge reached for the soap. He lathered his hands and began stroking them over Gage's chest, cleaning his skin and giving him a chance to recover.

"Shhh…," Forge said. "Sex is one thing, but being together, like this, naked and exposed, holding each other, just being together, is in some ways more intimate. Sex covers up the fact that when we're together, unclothed, we're showing ourselves to each other." Forge stepped back, letting go of Gage, and slowly turned in a circle. "This is me." He held his hands still. "After I married Granger, I didn't expect to ever show myself to anyone else." The water coursed down his back, and Forge stood still. "But then again, maybe he never really saw me."

"I see you," Gage told him. "I see the handsome man in front of me, the one who has the courage of a pack of lions. Not everyone will strip themselves bare in front of another person, and I don't mean just taking off their clothes." He moved forward, lightly touching Forge's chest above his heart. "I know what's here because you showed it to me years ago, and it's always inside you. The biggest heart I've ever met. I think that's why it hurt so much when I didn't hear from you. I thought that I'd lost the one thing I'd never find again—you."

Gage pressed to him, holding Forge tightly, their bodies entwining as the water washed over the two of them. "Just so you know, I will not lose you again. I will do whatever it takes to make sure you stay in my life. It nearly ripped me apart when I didn't get the letters you sent."

"And I thought you didn't love me." Forge could admit now that he'd rebounded, and after thinking Gage didn't want him, he'd gone out looking and found Granger. They'd been good together for a number of years, but now Forge saw that the two of them had never been great together. They hadn't been intuitive or known what the other needed. They'd worked at their relationship and talked about things. That was how they'd made things work. But when that communication had broken down, there wasn't anything deeper to fall back on. So they'd both retreated into their work, and eventually Granger had found what he thought he needed from someone else.

"I never stopped. Not even after all these years." Gage ran his hands down Forge's back to cup his butt. "You've been back in my life for just a few days, and already I'm more alive than I have been in years. Like I said, no matter what happens, I have no intention of giving you up. I'll fight for you just like I should have done seventeen years ago. I should have looked you up. I should have found you and talked to you."

"That's what we both should have done. We accepted what we thought happened and moved on. There were telephones and things. We could have found each other if either of us had looked beyond what we thought. It wasn't your fault, any more than it was mine." He rested his head on Gage's shoulders, kissing and licking the base of his neck. "You taste really good."

Gage lifted him off his feet, and Forge wound his legs around Gage's waist as Gage turned around to press him to the tile. His strong hands cradled Forge's ass, fingers teasing their way closer to his opening. He groaned and nearly bit Gage when he stroked over his sensitive skin. Gage's hand left him, followed by a soft click. "What are…?" Forge gasped when Gage's finger breached him. Forge tightened his grip on Gage with his legs, desperate for more.

"I want you. Now." Gage pressed him harder against the tile and lowered him. Gage's cock slid to his opening, and Forge rested his head back on the tile, gritting his teeth as he sank lower and Gage pressed into him.

"Oh God. I want." Forge held on to Gage with everything he had, sinking deeper, and Gage filled him more and more with every press. "So full." It was all he could gasp as Gage pressed upward and Forge sank the rest of the way, taking all of Gage inside.

"Is this okay?" Gage asked.

"If you stop, I'm going to bite the hell out of you," he growled. "Does it sound like this isn't okay?" He held Gage tighter. "Now fuck me like you mean it. Like you've wanted to for all those years." Forge groaned, and Gage bounced him up and down, grinding into him with the energy and fury of seventeen years of pent-up longing that Forge had waited just as long as Gage to release.

"I don't want to hurt you."

"The only way you'll hurt me is if you stop." Forge leaned in to kiss Gage hard and moaned as Gage drove him to the moon, which didn't take long. Forge was already so keyed up that it wasn't long before he teetered on the edge.

"That's it," Gage breathed. "Let me see you and feel you go to pieces." Gage held him tighter and thrust deep. Forge's entire body felt like it was going to burst into flame, and then he stilled and came with a shout that echoed off the bathroom walls. He breathed deeply, and Gage eased him down onto his feet, slipping from inside his body. He positioned Forge under the water, and Forge clung to Gage, steading himself as the water washed away the remnants of his excitement.

Gage held him up, and once Forge got his feet under him, Gage washed him gently, caressing his body as though it were precious. Then he turned off the water and helped him out of the shower, wrapped Forge in a huge towel, and guided him to the other room.

Forge made it to the bed and flopped down, completely wrung out. "What did you do to me?"

Gage leaned over him, gently caressing his cheek. "I wanted you to know that you are loved."

"Holy shit." Forge pulled Gage closer, holding him as he closed his eyes and dozed off. He knew they didn't have forever and had to get ready, but he needed a few minutes to get himself together or else he'd show up at Gage's parents' looking completely debauched. Hell, that was still a possibility with the way he felt at the moment. Maybe if he lay here with Gage next to him for the next few hours, which they didn't have, he'd be ready to go. "Is it stupid of me to be afraid to go to your parents'?"

"What are you scared of?" Gage asked.

"I don't know. We're going to the home of people who might be mixed up with the ones who killed Granger. I know they're your mom and dad, but what if they're behind all this and they take me into some dark room and have some huge guy soften me up before they really torture me and want information I don't have, then… then they take me out back, fit me for concrete boots, and I disappear in the bottom of the Chicago River?"

Gage pulled him closer. "Don't you think you're overreacting just a little?"

"I don't know." The truth was, he knew he was being silly, but Forge also had the feeling that something was going to happen tonight. This didn't seem right to him. Maybe he was being stupid and letting his imagination run away with him, but maybe there was something to it. "Just don't leave me."

"I won't. I promised I'd not let you go, and that certainly means not leaving you alone with my mother and father if I can help it. Hell, if you spend enough time with them, I'm afraid you'll end up running away screaming and never look back."

Forge was sure that wasn't going to happen. He slowly got up off the bed and opened the bags of clothes they'd purchased. He began taking off the tags and laying them out so he could get dressed, trying like hell to shake the sense of impending doom.

CHAPTER 6

GAGE SIGHED as he turned onto the road he'd grown up on and drove to the familiar driveway, which was filled with cars. He pulled in, and the valet his parents had hired for the evening opened the door and took the keys to park the car for them.

"Holy cow," Forge said as he got out, looking at the huge stone house with its portico and manicured yard. Most of the time Gage didn't notice it. This was just where he'd grown up, at least for the better part of his childhood.

"Yeah. Mom and Dad bought it when I was about ten. Mom wanted someplace where she could entertain to help further Dad's business. There's a full two and a half acres with a pool in the backyard. Dad likes to swim, so Mom put one in." He motioned Forge toward the front door.

"Are you sure we look okay?" Forge asked, stopping to fuss with his shirt for the twentieth time.

"You look amazing, so stop worrying. Remember, we're here for one reason." Gage patted Forge lightly on the lower back and rang the doorbell. After a few seconds, the door opened and his mother stood in front of him, looking as radiant as ever, wearing a dark blue designer blouse and perfectly pressed, flowing tan pants. The outfit accentuated the narrow waist that his mother cultivated at the gym with a fervor most people reserved for weekly visits to church. "Hello, Mom."

"Gage." She smiled, but it was slightly forced. "I'm glad you could come." She motioned them inside and closed the door.

"This is Forge. A close friend of mine." He smiled and could tell his mother was trying to deduce any meaning she could from what he'd just said. Gage wanted to tell her that, yes, they were sleeping together and that Forge was that kind of friend. But keeping her off-balance was to his advantage, so he kept quiet and kissed her cheek. "Is the party out back?"

"Yes. We're around the pool. Your father is grilling and telling some of his awful stories." She looked him over, seemed to find him acceptable, and led the way, even though Gage was well acquainted with the house.

"How are things, Mom?"

"Your father and I are doing well."

"How's business?" he asked, and her step faltered for just a second as she approached the door to the back patio. Most people wouldn't have noticed, but Gage was watching for any reaction. "I know things have been tough for some."

"Everything is great. Your father and I are making plans to turn the company over to the management team so we can spend more time together."

"That's really good. You and Dad deserve the chance to have some fun and get away." Gage stopped, with Forge standing next to him. His mother turned with a glare that softened when she seemed to realize that what Gage had said was the truth. "You and Dad worked hard for a lot of years, and you deserve a chance to relax and enjoy what you worked for." Spying his father through the glass, Gage opened the door and stepped outside.

Gage knew many of the people who'd gathered here from other parties and get-togethers his mother had thrown over the years. Some he knew from newspaper stories and television news reports, and their presence sent off bells in the back of his head.

"Son," his father said carefully as he handed the grilling utensils to one of the young men most likely serving dinner.

"It's good to see you, Dad." Gage shook his father's hand, and they shared a one-arm man-hug of sorts before stepping back. "This is Forge." They also shook hands, and Gage watched for any sign of recognition between them and was grateful when his dad's eyes sparked no recognition at all.

"What brings you to town?"

"Business," Gage answered, flicking his gaze over to the others in attendance. The small group of three standing slightly separate from the others worried him. Gage had never met any of them, but he knew *of* them. They were businessmen with reputations that were far less than stellar. His father was in the transportation business, and in Chicago, sometimes in order to survive, business was conducted with people one didn't necessarily want to work with. Gage knew his father had worked with sometimes shady people and managed those relationships for years without trouble. But now he was wondering if trouble had managed to slide in under the door.

His father must have followed his gaze. "They're customers."

"I see," Gage said slowly, feeling the tension rolling off his father. This wasn't good at all. His dad had always been the master of most every situation, and now it seemed he might have gotten in over his head. "Why don't you and I talk a little later." Gage paused to make sure his father understood before continuing. "It will be good to catch up. I've been so busy lately, I haven't had a chance to spend much time down here."

"That's a real shame," Mr. Abernathy, one of his father's longtime friends, said as he approached. Mr. Abernathy was a partner in the accounting firm his father's company used. Gage remembered playing with his son when he was a kid.

Gage smiled as he shook hands, then introduced Forge. "How's Doug?"

"Doug is great. He's out in California practicing law, showing me up with his success." Mr. A grinned proudly. "Marie and I were looking to retire out near them...." His smile faltered and he sighed.

"I'm so sorry about her. Mom called me and told me she'd passed. Mrs. A was a great lady." Marie Abernathy had been the person Gage had gone to when things with his own parents became too much. He was always welcome there, no matter what. "Are you still planning to relocate?"

"Doug and his wife want me to, and I'm seriously thinking about it. The firm will do well without me, and maybe it's time we realized we all need some time to ourselves." Mr. A looked square at his father. Whatever was going on, he seemed well aware of it. Gage hoped that at least meant his father hadn't stepped too far over the line.

"What kind of business brings you back?" Mr. A asked.

Gage put an arm around Forge's waist. Forge smiled, and Gage's dad hastily excused himself. "I'm looking into some things for a client." He wanted to keep Forge close even as he observed the others. Maybe Forge was right and coming here wasn't such a good idea. The three men kept watching them, and it didn't take Gage very long to realize they weren't looking at him as much as they were Forge.

"Business is good, then?" Mr. A asked as he too glanced over at the other men, tension rising all around them.

"Yes. People always need protection of some sort, especially when there are folks who don't understand the meaning of the word no." Gage glared at the men, challenging them, and he suppressed a smile when they turned away.

"Do you know them?" Mr. A asked in a low tone, and Gage shook his head. "Some new clients of your father's. I told him not to get involved with people like that. But…." Mr. A paused, and Gage glanced back to where his dad now stood next to his mother, the two of them talking softly. Then she plastered a familiar smile on her face and began mingling with the guests, specifically the men in question.

"I recognize them for who they are." Gage paused. "Do you need another drink? I think Forge and I could use one." He moved toward the bar to fix a drink for himself and Forge, holding Forge's hand as Mr. A followed. "Okay. Now I hope we can talk." Gage leaned in closer to Mr. A. "Is Dad's business in trouble? Is that why he's doing business with the likes of them?" He absently mixed some martinis, knowing it was Mr. A's drink of choice and hoping Forge liked them as well.

Mr. A spoke quietly as well. "Things aren't going well for your dad. He's slowing down, but he's in a tough, competitive environment that's growing more so every day, and it's taking more and more out of him to stay on top of the game. Something we all feel when we get to be our age." Mr. A lifted his glass, and Gage and Forge did the same. "Your dad thought these would be his golden years. He's worked all his life to provide for you and your mother, and now he's afraid he won't be able to do that and he's getting a little desperate."

"Okay. But has he done anything he can't undo? Has he gone beyond the point of no return?"

Mr. A sighed. "I don't believe so. You know your dad. He's a lion when it comes to business, but he'd never do anything shady or illegal."

Gage glanced at the contingent near the pool still talking with his mother. They were laughing, but the menace just from their presence hadn't diminished. "Then why are they here?"

"You'll have to ask your father that." Mr. A smiled and turned to Forge. "It was very nice to meet you." Then he returned to the others.

Gage stayed near the bar. He was beginning to think he was going to need a lot more to drink by the time this evening was over.

"They won't stop looking at me," Forge said quietly from behind him.

"I noticed that as well." Gage waited until his mother turned away, then whispered, "Time for a distraction. Ready?" When Forge nodded, he led Forge over to her. "Mom, Forge was just saying how lovely the house is."

Forge smiled, and as Gage expected, his mother went into preen mode, explaining all the hardships involved in getting the house "just right."

Gage left her to it and walked over to where the three men stood. "Nice evening, gentlemen," he said as he approached the group.

"Yes, it is." None of the men made any attempt at introduction. Obviously manners were not part of their training.

"I understand you and my father are contemplating doing business."

"So you're the son," the older gentleman said, obviously the one in charge, judging by the way the others stood just a few paces back.

"Yes. I have a security business…. I believe that's something we have in common." Gage met the leader's gaze. "Though mine is much more ethical and… shall we say… legal." He knew he was stirring a hornet's nest, but he needed to try to put them off their game, just a little.

"Do you know who this is?" one of the flanking men asked.

"Of course I do. Stanley Lucci. And I know who you are and work for. But this isn't a place where you're going to be able to do business."

Stanley stepped forward, his eyes as hard and dark as onyx. "I don't believe your father will have any choice." The antipathy and intimidation rolling off him were palpable. Gage saw his gaze flick to Forge and then back to him. "Neither does your friend."

Gage kept his cool while his mind flew at a rapid pace. "That depends on just how much information your father wants made public and how much heat he wants brought down on himself and your entire family." Gage stared right back, bluffing like hell, but he'd played enough poker in the service to know how to do it damn well. They might not have found all the information, but they had enough to be dangerous, and these guys didn't need to know they weren't in possession of all of it.

"That information can be deadly," Stanley said quietly, but with the same tone most people used to order a meal in a restaurant. Yet the threat hung there, or at least he meant it to.

"Maybe. But Granger didn't take the precautions I have. He was bound by ethics and codes of behavior because he was an

114

attorney, but we aren't. And those files you were looking for so diligently could easily find their way to the news media and then none of you will have a place to hide… anywhere." Gage kept his lips from curling upward when Stanley flinched. "So I expect you to call off your dogs and stand down. If anything happens to anyone I care about, we go nuclear, and you're going to be ground zero." He turned and walked away, not even looking back. He could feel their laser stares at his back, but he didn't care. They had to think he wasn't afraid of them. They were like bears—any show of fear and he would be dead.

His mother and Forge were still talking, which was better than Gage had hoped.

"What's going on?" his mother asked as the three guests slowly made their way over.

"I believe they have to be going, but want to thank you for the invitation." Gage turned, and all three of them said good night and did indeed thank his mother, explaining that something had come up and they had to leave. Gage grinned, and his mother visibly relaxed once they were gone.

Gage excused himself and went through the house to make sure his parents' guests left quietly and without incident. As he peered out the living room window, he saw the valets bring around a large black Mercedes, and the three men got inside. Stanley turned back, and Gage caught his eye, making sure Stanley knew Gage meant business. He watched until the car pulled away and was out of sight before returning to the party.

"Is everything okay?" Forge asked, hurrying toward him.

"Yes." Gage waited until Forge was close enough that he could speak without anyone overhearing. "But we need to find those files, and we need to do it fast. I played my cards and Stanley bought what I was saying, but he's going to test that I have the goods. And when he does, I have to be able to show that I have what I said I did and that I can bring the wrath of all that's holy down on the heads of his family, or none of us will ever be safe."

"Where did they go?" Gage's father asked.

"Something came up," Gage answered, then lowered his voice. "You and I need to talk after your guests leave." He met his father's gaze with the steeliest look he could muster. "This isn't negotiable."

"You come here to my house and give me orders." The volume was low, but the tone menacing.

"I just saved your life and your business." Gage wasn't going to back down, not for a second. "Maybe I should have let them worm their way into your company until you found yourself on the outside looking in and the company you built turned inside out and run into the ground. That's what people like that do." Gage could see he wasn't getting through and tried a different angle. "I'm here because they might be the ones who killed Forge's almost ex-husband, Granger. They executed him in his own backyard."

His father flinched. "You're sure about that?"

"I can't be sure of anything at this point. Now, go back to your guests, and we'll talk later. There are things we need to discuss." Gage waited until his father nodded, and then he found a seat on one of the patio sofas. Forge sat right next to him.

"I don't like it here. I feel so exposed, and those men aren't going to just back away. That isn't what they do."

"No, they aren't. But I can't just tell my parents to send everyone home. It will create more talk, and right now, we need a chance to think. We have to solve Granger's puzzle. The information we need is there, I know it is."

"I'll figure out that box, somehow," Forge said, and Gage threaded their fingers together.

HIS MOTHER and father said goodbye to the last of their guests a couple of hours later. His mother went to see about the cleanup, and Gage motioned his father and Forge into his dad's home office and closed the door.

"I need some answers, and I'm not going to beat around the bush. We found papers that indicate you took kickbacks or payoffs from the Luccis."

"No." His father stood behind his desk. "I never did. They offered payment, large ones, for some expedited shipments, but I didn't take them. I knew what they were trying to do and wanted no part of it."

"Then why were you doing business with them?"

His dad slumped into the chair. "Business has been tough lately, and I need more freight. They have plenty of legitimate business, and I was willing to work with them to try to garner some of it." He sighed. "Maybe that was me being naive."

"The records we found, which were in the hands of an attorney, showed those payments. Now, whether or not they were delivered, that isn't going to look good when they come out. Those people play by different rules, and sometimes people end up dead." Gage went over to where Forge had sat in one of the other chairs in the room and took his hand, knowing this was going to be upsetting for him. Everything about this situation sucked—well, everything except being able to hold Forge's hand and try to protect him.

His father's gaze zeroed in on where they touched, and his eyebrows cocked upward.

"Gage is someone special to me," Forge said rather softly.

"I see." His dad's reaction was hardly a ringing endorsement of acceptance.

"My relationships aren't the issue here. Forge and I are trying to get to the bottom of a situation, and you and Mom have become involved in it. Because of that you could be in danger." Gage closed his eyes and groaned. This was a real mess. "Why don't you and Mom take a vacation? Go somewhere for a few weeks. Get away and kind of disappear."

"What?" His father's voice boomed off the office walls.

"If what I think is correct, associates of your party friends may have killed Granger. They won't hesitate to go after you and Mom

117

if they think it's to their advantage. Call your security company, have them watch the house, and go on a trip."

His dad narrowed his gaze. "You're serious?"

"He's deadly serious," Forge said. "This isn't a game." He gripped Gage's hand tighter as tension ramped up to the ceiling.

"Trust me, Dad. These people aren't who you want to do business with. You said things have been tough, then do what you've always done in the past: innovate and come up with something new. It's what you're good at. Open a new market and take advantage of that opportunity. But don't sell your soul and do something you're going to regret."

"You should have been here to take over. It's—"

Gage shared a look with Forge, who nodded, pulled his hand back, then stood and quietly left the office. It amazed him that Forge seemed to know and understand what needed to happen without Gage saying a word. Forge closed the door, leaving Gage sitting across the desk from his father, exactly where he'd been when they talked about this subject the last time.

"Running your company isn't what I want to do. It never was. Building Livingston Cartage was your dream, not mine. I have my own, and it includes the man who just left. I know you have a tough time with that, but I'm not going to hide who I am or what I want."

"But it's my legacy."

Gage shook his head. "Your legacy is the relationships you leave behind, not some business. Don't you see that? I won't be tied to something just because you want it so badly. You have the right to dream and build whatever is going to make you and Mom happy. But you don't have the right to determine what will make me happy. Do you understand? Turn the company over to good managers and let them find the next opportunity if you aren't able to do it," he said, though he doubted very much that was true. After a pregnant pause where they both stared at each other, he added, "We're a lot alike."

"How do you figure that?" His father didn't look away, and Gage wouldn't expect him to.

"We're both stubborn as shit, for starters." He cocked his head, and his dad rolled his eyes and nodded. "I started my own business, Dad. I'm successful and damn good at what I do—the same as you. I wanted to do things my own way and follow my own path. Does that sound at all familiar to you?"

His dad huffed, and Gage could see his resolve fading. "But I wanted you to have a better life and more chances than what I had. I built the company. All you needed to do was take over and run it into the future."

"Instead, I went into the Army and then used my training to start my own company." Gage stood. "Don't you see it? I took after you and found my own way. I don't want to carry on your life—I want to build one of my own. Is that really so hard for you to understand?" He leaned over the desk, forcing his father to acknowledge what he was saying. "Or is all of this just a smoke screen for the fact that your son is gay and you can't deal with that either?" He pushed away, turned around, and stood tall. "Maybe it was a mistake coming here at all. You can go ahead and make all the stupid moves you want. Do business with gangsters and criminals. I have my own life and my own business."

"Gage—"

"You're too damned stubborn to listen or care what anyone else wants, so why should I bother with—"

"Gage!" His father cut through his rant, and Gage whirled around. "I think you made your point."

"Fine. What are you going to do about it?"

His father picked up the phone for his assistant and asked her to make a hotel reservation. Gage stepped forward and shook his head. His father paused in his speech, and Gage motioned for him to hang up.

"What? You wanted us to get away."

"Don't make a reservation. Just show up and check in. Pay cash and stay out by the airport. There are a lot of hotels, and people come and go all the time. Then decide where you and Mom want to go, buy plane tickets, and just get away. I need to figure all this out, and I don't want to worry that they'll use you to try to get to me… to Forge and me. Call me each day to let me know you're okay." Gage reached into his wallet and pulled out his card. "This is a secure line, and Margie will get word to me that you're fine. Don't tell any of your friends where you are."

His father took the card. "What about work?"

"Buy a new computer and use that. It will be clean and untraceable for a period of time. Again, tell no one where you are, and watch your back."

His dad stood, eyes darting around the room in the first show of nervousness Gage had seen. "You really think your mother and I could be in danger?"

"Those people don't take no for an answer. Dad, they thought they had you on the hook, and they aren't just going to let you go if they can help it. I need some time to unravel this puzzle and do my best to make sure they can't hurt you or Forge ever again. I'm not sure how I'm going to do all that yet, but I need to know you and Mom are safe. So just go. Call the security service, then lock up the house and get out of here. If you've got any cash in the house, use that. If not, get some. Don't use credit cards or anything that can be traced. Stay with friends you can trust if you'd like."

"I have some cash in the safe."

"Then get it. Pack bags and put them in the trunk of the car. Oh, and make sure you have the security company check the system on the property. Tell them you think it's been compromised. They need to make sure there aren't any honey hooks into the system."

"Okay. How do I tell your mother all this?" He lowered himself back into his chair.

"Just tell her the way you tell her everything else. You and Mom have always been a team, so handle this the same way. You know Mom. She loves an adventure. After all, she put up with us for all these years." Gage smiled, and his father did the same. It was the first time in years that they'd both seemed contented in each other's company. "Now I think I need to rescue Forge from the grand inquisitor."

His dad nodded, and Gage turned to go. "Are you serious about that young man or is he just a friend?"

Gage paused at the door. "Dad, he's the other half of my soul. I knew that when I first met him when I was in the Army hospital." There was no need to bring up old wounds, not when he and his dad had made progress. "Forge and I lost touch back then. But we found each other now. I know you don't understand the whole gay thing. But it's the same as you and Mom. I love him and will move mountains to keep him happy."

His dad sighed. "Then that's how it should be."

Gage opened the door and went in search of his mother. He found her and Forge in the kitchen, sitting at the table with a drink in front of each of them. When he'd brought Forge, the last thing he'd expected was for him to hit it off with his mother. Maybe there was such a thing as miracles after all.

His mother looked up at his approach. "Forge was telling me that you knew each other in the service."

"Yes. We met back then but lost touch. Forge sent me letters, but I never got them." He held Forge's hand and watched his mother for any reaction, but only saw the slightest flinch around her eyes. She might not have consciously made the connection, but somewhere inside, he thought her conscience jabbed her.

"Gage....," she whispered, looking between the two of them, her eyes darting from one to the other.

"Yes, Mom. He sent the letters to the house, but I never got them." He let the implications hang in the air and waited while her mind wound through her own actions.

Gage saw the moment she remembered. Her eyes widened and she gasped softly. Then the mask she usually wore when she was in society and encountered something unpleasant slid into place.

"I know what you did." He wasn't letting her get away with it. Not that there was anything that could change the past. It was what it was, and hanging on to the hurt was never going to help.

"Gage, I—"

"It's in the past, and through some miracle of fate, we found each other again." Gage held Forge's hand tighter. "Forge and I need to go." He turned to his dad, who had just walked in from his office. "Please do what I asked." He'd had all of his mother and father that he could take at the moment. Gage didn't want to hold what had happened against them. "Call me to let me know you're safe."

"Harry, what's going on?" his mother asked, standing as Gage gently tugged Forge out of the room and toward the front door.

"Shirley, just go sit down and I'll explain."

Gage turned, and his father met his gaze and nodded. At least he could breathe a little easier knowing his parents would be safe.

He closed the door to the house and looked around carefully. Gage had the feeling they might be watched, but the hair on the back of his neck didn't stand up. Still, he wasn't going to take any chances. "Let's get to the car and back to the hotel. It's late." The valet was waiting for them and handed Gage the keys.

"Did anyone get near the car at all this evening?" Gage asked.

"No. Why would they?" he answered, and Gage handed him a twenty before getting in. Once Forge was inside, Gage pulled out of the circular drive and onto the quiet suburban street. He took multiple turns and made certain he wasn't followed before driving anywhere near the hotel where they were staying. Finally he pulled into the parking lot, and they went up to their room.

"Will they be able to find us here?" Forge asked once they were behind closed doors.

"No. I didn't check in under my own name. Over the years I've developed a number of alternate identities, and I used one of them. I'm very good at what I do, and believe it or not, it's very easy to get a credit card in any name you choose. So, unless they know the name I registered under, we're safe enough for now.

We also used the underground garage so they're going to have to specifically look for our car." Gage sat on the edge of the bed as Forge picked up the bag containing the jade box and sat next to him. He took it out and turned it over in his hands, a soft rattle coming from inside.

"There's a way to open this. I have to find it. Granger told me that there is usually a piece that presses inward and starts the cascade of movement that allows them to open."

"Okay. But what if it's a piece you have to pull out? The box is small, so there isn't going to be much room to push anything inward." Gage extended his hand, and Forge placed the box in it. He turned it over, lifting the box so he could look the dragon in the eyes.

"I don't think he can look back," Forge quipped, laughing. He reached for the box and gasped slightly before gently taking it and pulling the tail of one of the dragons, which moved outward slightly before coming to a complete stop. "That's it." Forge carefully moved the remaining pieces until the side of the box lowered and the lid slid off to the side.

"What's in it?"

Forge placed another thumb drive in Gage's hand, along with a folded piece of paper.

Gage opened the page, read it briefly, and then turned to Forge. "This is for you." He stood to give Forge a chance to read the note. "From the date, it was written six months ago."

Forge took the page and read aloud.

"Dear Forge,

"If you're reading this note, then I'm dead and the precautions I took to try to save myself—and by extension, you—weren't enough. The last few months have been difficult for us, and my work has been suffering. I know it's because I can't concentrate, and the two of us arguing about everything has gotten me to the point that I can't think straight most of the time. I want you to know that none of what's happened is your fault. I know it was mine because I was weak."

Forge sniffed and looked up from the page, wiping his eyes. At Gage's nod, he continued.

"I know you have no reason to believe me. I know I was weak, but I was also set up, and since I thought I was too smart to let that happen, it's exactly what did happen. Then you found out, or they arranged for you to find out. I don't know which, but hurting you brought my world to an end. Like I said, everything is all my fault, I know that. I should have been stronger.

"The people who set me up have no scruples and will do anything to get what they want. I'm willing to bet they think they can find what they want, but they can't. My computer was encrypted, and they will never find the key. If they destroy it, they're wasting their time. Everything needed to bring them down is in cloud storage, but you need the access information. You have what you need. You know the private account, and I put the password where we kept our personal papers. You just need to look for it.

"I know you and I had a good life and I was the one who changed all that. But know that I regret it. Be safe, and above all, be happy."

Forge wiped his eyes. "I wonder how much of this was still true after all these months." Forge refolded the letter and placed it gently on the bed. He didn't move, sitting quietly, staring at the wall. "Things between us got so messed up."

"Maybe. But at least you know that Granger did care and felt bad for what happened."

"Six months ago. He put all that crap in a letter instead of sitting down and talking to me. We were living in the same house, avoiding each other, and all he needed to do was try to talk and explain. I don't know if I'd have been able to forgive him right away… or take him back, but we could have talked instead of arguing about everything we owned for the last six months and getting nowhere."

"I bet you weren't getting anywhere because Granger was still holding on." Gage took Forge's hand, lightly stroking the back with his thumb. "I know he was a lawyer, but sometimes people don't have the words for what they want, so they act on their emotions instead. Maybe he hoped things could work out if he kept the two of you living together as long as possible." He continued stroking Forge's hand and caught his gaze. "Are you going to be okay?"

"Yes. I'm surprised to see the note, and yet I think I understand. I always thought of Granger as the kind of man who was always in control and knew what he wanted." Forge tugged his hand away and put both over his face. "Ten years and I didn't understand who he really was." He gasped and wiped his eyes. "Granger wasn't the person I thought because I didn't see beyond the mask that he wanted everyone to see. He wanted to be the strong, in-charge, amazing lawyer. So he played that part, even for me." Forge picked up the note once again. "But this shows me something different, something I should have seen and never did." He set the letter down and wiped his eyes once again.

"But he didn't want you to see anything else," Gage tried to explain, but Forge shook his head.

"I know you have this image of the strong protector, and you are that, but you're also gentle and the most caring person I've ever met. You're strong because you help others be strong. I saw who you were almost immediately, but I never really saw Granger."

"Did he see you?" Gage asked, and Forge grew quiet, shrugging.

"I thought he did. But maybe not." Forge leaned closer, and Gage put his arm around him. Forge sighed. "I'm sorry about what happened to Granger. He didn't deserve to die." Forge picked up the letter. "Though he did think it was a possibility."

"Yes, he did. But no one deserves to have their life taken away like that. And somehow we're going to make those responsible pay for what they did." Gage gestured at the paper and Forge handed it to him. Gage read it through again. "He says you'll know the information you need."

"Yeah. I'm pretty sure I know what email address he's referring to. Granger had one that he used only for the most personal communications. He rarely gave it out except to close friends. Most of the time he directed communications to his work email so his assistant could help deal with it. He said the password was where we kept our personal papers, but that's the safe we already went through."

"Then we need to look again." Gage patted Forge's hand. "We're going to need to go back to your house and see what we can find. I'll call Harv in the morning just to check that everything has been quiet, but he would have called if he'd seen anything."

Forge picked up the flash drive out of the box, holding it in his hand. "I wonder what this is."

Gage got his computer, booted it up, and inserted the drive. He waited for it to start, and then pictures flashed on the screen. Forge stared, mesmerized by the images of him and Granger. The first pictures showed a much younger Forge, closer to the one from Gage's memories. Skiing, boating, a cruise with glaciers in the background. This was obviously something Granger had put together to document his and Forge's life as a couple. The slide show continued, with the two of them getting older and ending with a photograph of them in tuxedos, a cake in front of them, holding champagne glasses.

"You had a good life together," Gage said softly.

"Yes."

But it was over, and the grief showed in Forge's eyes. Gage held him tighter, and Forge turned his face to his shirt. Gage squeezed him and let Forge release the grief he'd been holding for days. He had no illusions that Forge needed to grieve for the life he'd thought he had. Gage was glad that Forge and Granger had been happy, for the most part. He hated thinking that Forge had truly been miserable.

"Granger and I had good times together, and I did love him and he loved me. In the end things went to hell, but that still doesn't mean that we hadn't cared about each other." Forge held him tighter. "Now it's all over, and we can't say the things to each other that we want to." He gasped, and Gage slowly rocked him back and forth. "Everything between us ends like this. There's no chance to say we're sorry and no chance to forgive in return."

"You can always forgive him. Granger will know. And maybe that's what you need to do so you can truly move on."

"Eight months of fighting and arguing was more than enough for that," Forge countered.

Gage lightly stroked Forge's cheek. "It isn't, and deep down you know that. The fighting was only the outward sign of something else. If you cared enough to fight, then there's still some feeling there."

"True, but I had given up and was about to walk away when I found Granger in the backyard. I'd told Vince to settle, that I wanted to be able to move on with my life." Forge turned to him. "We were good together for a while, but things were over between us." Forge sighed. "That part of my life is over. It was kind of Granger to write the note, and it made me feel better, but only about moving on."

Forge turned toward him, and Gage realized he'd been holding his breath and was likely to turn blue. He'd been worried that the note from Granger was going to open up a whole new round of soul searching. Not that Gage could blame Forge for a second. The note had been powerful; even he'd felt that.

"Maybe we should get ready to try to sleep," Gage offered.

"Yeah. I never thought days could be so packed with activity." Forge yawned, and Gage motioned for him to use the bathroom first. While he was gone, Gage lowered the lights and pulled down the bed covers. He took the chance to undress and figured he'd take his turn once Forge was done.

The door opened and Forge stepped out, bare, only for Gage to see and drink in. The view was stunning, like in the movies where the character has been hiding and then shows their true self and it blows you away. That was his Forge, beautiful chest, narrow hips, and eyes the color of the brightest sky. Forge came closer, and Gage's mouth went dry. It never ceased to amaze him how Forge could do that each and every time.

"Do you need a turn?" Forge asked without looking away.

Gage shook his head, unable to take his gaze off the splendid creature in front of him. Gage lowered himself to the bed, sitting on the edge, willing Forge to come forward. As soon as he was close enough, Gage placed his hands on his hips and drew Forge into his embrace, sliding his hands around to the perfect globes of Forge's butt. He squeezed and brought his lips to Forge's belly, inhaling the deep, masculine richness of his skin before kissing it, the muscles under his lips fluttering.

"You are so beautiful." Gage closed his eyes, inhaling again. "I waited so long for this." It seemed like a lifetime, and now his spirit soared with every look, each touch, making his heart beat faster. Gage hadn't realized how much he'd put the emotional and caring portion of himself on hold until Forge released it.

"So have I." Forge ran his fingers through Gage's hair, and Gage shivered at the roughness for even the slight pull of his hair. It didn't hurt in the least, but the movements were strong and confident, with nothing tentative. "I mean, I know you had other relationships. Not that I want to hear about them now…."

Gage chuckled. He certainly didn't want to talk about any other men at this moment. "I told you. There was no one who touched my heart. I had men in my life, but things never lasted very long." Gage wound his arms around Forge's waist and muscled him onto the bed.

Forge laughed as Gage pressed him onto the mattress, the smile worth everything he possessed. "That's a long time to feel unloved."

Gage climbed on top of Forge, staring deeply into his now darkened eyes. "How can anyone, ever, compare to you?" He knew Forge would argue, so Gage kissed him and didn't let up. He wasn't in the mood to hear anything contrary, and after a few breathlessly intense moments, it seemed Forge had lost the will to argue. "You were all I ever wanted, and I thought it better to be alone than to settle. And that's what I would have been doing. I looked for that spark, that gentle touch that wrapped around my soul, but I never felt it with anyone."

Forge stroked his cheek before wrapping his arms around Gage's neck. "Why not?"

"I think it's because of what I went through. When I couldn't move my hands or legs, you sat beside me. You didn't do it out of pity, but because you cared. You saw me at my most helpless and defenseless and made me feel alive. You, Forge, gave me something to look forward to each day, when all I wanted to do was kill myself." Gage closed his eyes, trying to keep his emotions from overwhelming him. "You loved me for who I was then, at my worst. No one else can ever do that. The guys I've met since I got out of the Army have all seen me as I am now. They didn't know what's on the inside, and none of them can ever understand it. They don't know the pain, determination, and guts it took to be able to walk again, or the thrill we shared when I was able to move my hands. You do because you saw me and cared for me."

Forge shrugged slightly. "I only did what anyone would do."

"No, you didn't, and don't ever say that to me. You brought me back to life, nurtured my spirit and my heart. I needed that before I could begin to heal physically." Gage leaned closer, capturing Forge's lips. Sometimes words were just not adequate, and Gage set out to show Forge just what he'd done all those years ago meant to him.

CHAPTER 7

FORGE WOKE to near complete quiet. The morning sun peered around the edges of the curtains, and he was alone in the bed. Forge sat up, the covers pooling around his waist. "Gage?" he said softly, and the bathroom door opened, light spilling out, then going off once again.

"I didn't want to wake you," Gage said softly. "I called Harv, and the house has been quiet. Margie has been monitoring the cameras and reports that the office has been quiet as well. Apparently they've given up for the time being, or they're saving what they have for later."

"Are we going home?"

"Yes," Gage answered, walking over to sit on the edge of the bed in only a pair of plain white briefs. "We need to find out some answers, and we need to do it quickly."

"Detective Coleridge is going to be mad as hell…."

"You promised you'd tell him what was in the box, and you're going to do that. If he wants to see what was inside, you can show him everything. It might help him crack the code on the computer, though I don't think so."

"What about the online backups?" Forge yawned, and Gage leaned closer to him.

"I only want to keep you safe. That's what I'm here for. If the police can do that by taking down the entire operation, that's fine with me. As long as you're safe." He put his arm around Forge, and Forge wrapped his around Gage's middle and held tightly.

"I feel safe when you're around. But you can't be there forever." Forge clung to Gage with everything he had, trying not to shake out of sheer fear. "Well, maybe you can, but you can't keep me safe forever. No one will be able to. So maybe I should turn over everything I have and will ever have to the police and leave town, maybe the country. I could try to start over somewhere else." That wasn't what he wanted at all. Forge wanted his life back— well, some life back, one he could live happily again. Every time he closed his eyes and pictured what he wanted, he saw Gage and him together. The funny thing was, he never saw the two of them together at his house, but at the rooms in Gage's office.

"Don't be hasty. Let's go back and see if we can't crack this thing open, then figure out what we're going to do with what we find."

Gage kissed him, and Forge let go of his worries for an hour or so, Gage taking him to a place where they didn't matter at all. After making love, they showered together once again, Gage cleaning him gently and massaging away the aches he knew he'd feel for days regardless of how much hot water they used.

"Go ahead and get dressed," Gage said softly, wiping his back with one of the soft towels. "I'm going to shave. I'll be right out."

Forge dressed in a hurry and was glad Gage was out of sight. Watching Gage running around bareassed got his motor running again, and Forge wasn't sure he was ready for another round so soon. Gage emerged as he was finishing, and Forge perved on him a little as he dressed and gathered their things together in the shopping bags. He also packed Gage's computer into his bag and set everything by the door. When they were ready, they marched out of the room to the elevator. Gage settled the bill at the desk, and without wasting a minute, they were down to the car and out onto the streets of Chicago.

"Just like before, use your mirror to watch for anyone behind us."

"What if there's another tracker on the car?" Forge asked, and Gage pointed Forge to the onboard display.

"This car is newer, and we installed some special programming so it checks itself for any signals emanating from the car. There's the GPS signal and nothing more." Gage patted his leg. "But I like that you're thinking that way. It will help keep you safe." He turned at the next corner, and Forge checked the mirror. It was difficult to see since they were in heavy city traffic, but it didn't look like they were being followed.

Once they reached the highway, Gage went north, and Forge continued checking behind them. No one stayed near them for very long, and after a while with every car passing them, Gage sped up and they headed toward home.

Forge grew more excited and anxious the closer they got to the house. Was it going to be all right and was he going to be safe there? He certainly hoped so.

"We aren't going to sleep at the house. We'll keep watching it, but it will be safer at the office," Gage told him as though he were reading Forge's mind. "We'll get everything out of the safe and take it back there. I have secure internet connections, and we can try to work out what Granger meant from there."

"If you think so." Forge had been looking forward to sleeping in his own bed, but if Gage thought they'd be safer at the office, he'd do what he said. "Will I be able to get into my work email?"

"Certainly," Gage answered. "I suggest you call Detective Coleridge and let him know where we've been and what you found. He'll probably want to meet us at the house, and that will add an extra layer of protection, at least for a while. When we're there, assume that we're being watched and that someone can hear what we're saying. You were spied on before, so it will probably happen again."

Forge thought Gage might be overreacting, but he nodded and grew quiet, looking out the window as they passed through downtown. Forge watched the old brewery buildings pass as they continued their way north. Then he made his call and was lucky enough to be connected right away. "Detective, its Forge Reynolds, and I was able to figure out how to open the jade box."

"Where have you been?" Coleridge practically shouted, sounding partially relieved and partially pissed.

"Chicago. After being followed and people trying to run us off the road, we thought getting out of town might be best. Did you get anything from the men in the car?"

"I'll meet you at the house and you can bring me up to date, and I'll do the same. We've made some progress on our end, and it sounds like you've done likewise." He seemed in a hurry. "How long before you can get there?"

"Twenty minutes, tops." Forge didn't tell him that Gage had someone watching the house. "We'll see you then, and it might be best if you made a show of coming over. Please don't be subtle. There are people still after us. You making a show of force might be more than a little helpful."

"I understand. Tell me all about it when I get there." He hung up, and Forge put his phone in his pocket.

Gage called Harv to let him know what was happening, and he agreed to stay out of sight. Forge held the bag with the jade box on his lap until they pulled into the driveway, where a police cruiser was already parked.

"Was this conspicuous enough?" Detective Coleridge said as he got out of the car.

"Yes. Thank you." Forge carried the bag with the box to the door and unlocked it. He let Coleridge enter first and check out the house before going inside. Gage followed the others, and they sat at the table while Coleridge checked out the office once more before removing the tape so Forge could begin putting the room back in order.

"What did you find?" Coleridge sat down.

Forge worked the mechanism to open the box and handed Coleridge the note and the drive. "There's just a slide show on there with pictures of Granger and me. As you can see from the note, he was aware for some time that he was working with dangerous people. I think he gathered the files we've been looking for in order to protect himself, but instead he brought on his death."

"Have you found the files?"

"No. But I believe they're in the cloud storage he had." Forge pointed to the note. "I think I know the email he's referring to, but I haven't found the password. The last time we went through the safe, I found nothing I wasn't expecting and certainly nothing that said what his passwords were." Forge looked to Gage.

"In some papers we found in Granger's office," Gage explained, pulling out the pages from the hidden drawer in Granger's desk, "we found references to my father. When we were in Chicago, I spoke with him. My dad didn't take any payoffs, but we believe the information we are searching for is on the Lucci family."

Detective Coleridge didn't seem surprised. "The men chasing you were identified as having ties to the Lucci family. They lawyered up quickly, and all we could really get them on was a traffic violation. They weren't going to admit chasing you, and their lawyers were damn good."

"I was afraid of that," Gage said. "When we were at my father's last night, Stanley Lucci was there with two of his men. They were trying to put pressure on my father to do business with them, but I gave them a very clear message."

"Where are your parents now?"

"Taking a vacation. I don't know where they are, but I got a message from my father a few hours ago that they were boarding a plane for Europe and planned to stay a few weeks. Hopefully they'll be out of their grasp until we can clear all this up." Gage took Forge's hand, holding it under the table. "The Lucci family is involved…."

"That's what I figured. They have their fingers in many pies, and it's going to be nearly impossible to take them down. Their business goes through many people, and they rarely do their own dirty work. Though they're good at intimidation."

Forge had no idea what they were going to do other than try to find the information Granger had. "You said you'd made progress."

"We were able to unlock the laptop with the help of federal agencies. But the files we need have additional encryption, and we don't have the key to unlock them. Do you suppose it could be this same password he refers to in his note?"

"I don't know," Forge answered. "I'll go get what's in the safe again, but I don't think there's anything in there. Remember that Granger wrote that note six months ago, and he could have removed whatever he put that password on, which would be the end of it. There weren't any notes or handwritten cards with some mysterious password on it. Besides, Granger would never do that. It wasn't like him at all. He loved puzzles, so he'd put it somewhere that wasn't obvious."

Forge left the room and went downstairs to open the safe and transfer everything to a box, then carried it all back up. He set the box on the table and stepped back, letting Coleridge take a look at some of the personal items from his and Granger's marriage. Forge sat down and let Coleridge do what he needed to.

Coleridge went through everything systematically, looking and then putting the items aside. Once he was done, Forge put the things back in the box and returned them to the safe, locked it up, and covered it the way it had been before.

"That seems like a dead end."

"I'm afraid it is. Like I said, I know the account email, but the password truly seems lost to all of us. The note is six months old. Maybe Granger changed the password and took the card out of the safe, but didn't change what he'd put in the safe-deposit box." Forge handed Coleridge the papers they'd found. "You're going to have to make do with these. It's all we have at the moment."

"Unfortunately not everything on those pages is true," Gage added, pointing out the information about his father.

"You believed your dad?"

Gage nodded. "He and I haven't gotten along very well lately, but he was surprised I knew the information and he swears he never took anything from them that could be a bribe. Who knows?"

Detective Coleridge stood, then paced across the room. "We aren't getting anywhere very quickly. Every time we run down a lead, we hit a dead end. We need to find this information that Granger was keeping." Frustration rolled off him, and Forge felt every ounce of it. Forge deserved answers—they all did—and there were so many questions still hanging in the air.

"How did he get messed up with these people?" Forge asked. "He had a good practice that was well respected."

"They prey on weakness of any sort. I don't know what Granger's was, but they took advantage of him. You said he cheated on you. And his note said that he was set up."

"Yeah. Things with Granger and me had been difficult for a while, but we were trying to work things through. At least that's what I thought until I found out about the affair. Granger said he wanted someone younger, but it didn't last."

"Sounds to me like Granger might have been played."

Forge nodded and looked at the floor. "I keep wondering if I'd been more of what he needed, then this wouldn't have happened." A wave of guilt as high as the ceiling washed over him. "I should have been more vigilant. I took Granger for granted and thought he'd always be there. Then he wasn't, and what we had was gone. Now he isn't coming back."

Coleridge sat across from him. "These feelings are normal, but there was nothing you could do. If Granger was being played, then they already figured out that things were strained between you and played on Granger's weakness. Regardless of how they did it, what happened isn't your fault. You're the victim of a crime, and unfortunately this is how many victims feel over time."

Forge looked to Gage, who nodded slowly. "You didn't do this, and you aren't responsible for what happened with Granger and what he did." Gage turned to Coleridge. "What about the body?"

"We'll release it today. I don't think there's anything more that we can learn from it."

Forge nodded blankly. "I'll call his parents, and they can make arrangements. They blame me for what happened. I know it isn't my fault, at least in my head. I keep telling myself that, but in my heart, I—" Forge groaned and sat back in his seat. "What the hell is wrong with me?"

"Nothing at all. Your husband was killed in the most violent way possible, and we aren't any closer to finding out who did it or why." Coleridge took the papers they'd given him and left the house.

Forge stared at Gage, wondering what they were going to do next. "We're done for," he said. "Those people from Chicago are going to figure out that we don't have the information you said we did and they're going to come after us, and then that's going to be the end of it." Forge got to his feet, running a hand through his hair. "Maybe we should just tell them the information Granger had is locked away and they don't have anything to worry about. Their deep, dark secrets are safe from everyone and they can back off."

Gage shook his head. "Okay. Let's say that they believe us and agree to back off. What about Granger? They'll have gunned him down, and the person who did it will get off scot-free. I know he cheated, but did he deserve that?"

"No, he didn't. Not at all." Forge began pacing. "This is all one of Granger's puzzles. He said that the password was where he kept our personal papers stored, and that was always the floor safe. It's where we kept the wills and powers of attorney. Granger was always really anal that we have all those things. But we went through everything twice and came up with nothing at all."

"Like you said, the letter was written six months ago. What if he changed the password or pulled that information out of the safe because of what was happening between the two of you? There are a lot of things that could have changed. We have to face that."

"But we can't give up," Forge said. The thought of never knowing what truly happened to Granger would haunt him for the rest of his life.

"We're not going to. There is an answer to this riddle. We have to find it." Gage stood, stopped his pacing, and hugged him tightly. "Go on upstairs and pack yourself a bag. We're not going to stay here tonight."

Forge went up to his room and packed some clothes for a few days, then returned downstairs. Gage was on the phone with Margie, talking softly, but he hung up when Forge entered. He escorted Forge out of the house through the garage doors and to the car. Forge buckled himself in, and Gage drove them toward his office, making quite a few false turns, looking for anyone who might be following them. Forge didn't see anyone, and Gage pulled into the lot, used the remote to open the doors, and drove inside, the heavy-duty overhead door sliding down behind them.

"We should be safe here."

"I hope so." Forge's mind went back to yesterday and the way they'd been located the last time.

"Margie has been watching the property, and there hasn't been anything other than cursory interest since we sent them on their wild goose chase. They also have no way of knowing if we're here or not. We're completely out of sight and the entire facility looks deserted. Margie is working from home and watching over secure internet connections that are encrypted six ways from Sunday. We're safe. Besides, I doubt after they followed us here once, they'd think we'd return." Gage led him inside and through the office area to the small living quarters. "Go ahead and make yourself comfortable. I'm going to see what we have to eat. It's past lunchtime and we left Chicago in a hurry."

Forge's stomach rumbled at the thought of food. He set up his computer on the coffee table in the living area, booting it up. Gage poked his head in long enough to put in the passcode so Forge could access the internet, and he spent the next hour answering emails and working on paperwork. He had a load of meetings starting on Monday, but until then, work had cleared his schedule, which Forge was extremely grateful for.

"What are you thinking?" Gage asked as he came in with a bowl of soup and set it on the table where Forge was working.

"I don't know. I keep thinking that I want this all to be over, and then I wonder what will happen once it is. In the last few days, my world has been turned upside down, and I don't know what to do about it." Forge sat back, staring at the bowl of soup as though he wasn't sure what it was.

"What do you want?" Gage asked softly.

Forge shrugged. "I know I don't want you to disappear into the ether. I want to have my life settled and quiet once again." He blinked. "But I bet your life is never quiet."

"I have to admit, my life is rarely dull and I don't sit on one place for very long. I spend a lot of my time out in the field, helping people who need protection, just like I've been helping you. It's what I do and a big part of who I am and how I make my living."

Forge nodded slowly as what Gage was saying sank into his mind, chilling him. After this was over, Gage would go on to a new case and protect someone else. His life was going to be active and on the go all the time. He wasn't going to be able to slow down and take a nine-to-five job, coming home to Forge at the end of the day. Was Forge going to be able to handle that, and did Gage want to come home to him? Was Gage going to want to settle down with him and his relatively quiet life? Gage deserved someone who could keep up with him.

"Is that what you're worried about? That my life will be more than you can handle? Or that I'll want someone… different?" Gage sat next to him. "You need to remember that I looked for you in everyone I met for seventeen years. I don't know what our future will look like, but I do know that I want one with you. So let's get through the next few days, figure out what's going on, make sure you're safe, and then we can sit down and figure out the kind of life we want together."

Forge nodded but didn't move. "What if you get bored with me? It was pretty obvious that's what happened with Granger. We got settled in our lives and they became dull and something Granger didn't want anymore. What if that happens with you?"

Gage smiled and actually chuckled. Forge wanted to punch him for it. "I somehow doubt I could ever get bored with you." Gage took his hand. "You think my life is all excitement and one big adrenaline rush. Most of the time it's what Harv has been doing for the last few days—watching, waiting, and doing a whole lot of nothing." He leaned closer, and Forge's heart beat a little faster just because Gage closed the distance between them. "Besides, you are the most exciting thing to come into my life. You make my pulse race and make me gasp for air just by looking at me. I don't want to be without you. That's as simple as I can put it. When this is over, I want to come home and find you in my bed, waiting for me, just like you should have been for the last seventeen years. I want to hear your stories and have you listen to mine. I want to make love in the middle of the night when it's raining cats and dogs. I want to be there for you when you grow old and we end up sitting in rocking chairs on our porch somewhere where it's warm and peaceful." Gage paused and stared into Forge's eyes. "I don't know exactly what our lives will look like once we're together—we'll figure it out—but I know I do want to have a life with you. I always have." Gage held him tightly, as though he were the most precious person in the world. It had been so very long since he'd felt that way that Forge almost wondered if he could even remember.

"I want that too. But what if—"

"You and I can do whatever we want. Hell, the doctors didn't think I'd be able to walk again, but you and I… well, we showed them all those years ago, and if we can do that, then we can do anything." Gage pressed him back on the sofa, and Forge forgot about food or being hungry. All that mattered was Gage next to him.

Forge clung to him. "I want you with me, like this, all the time."

"It's what I want too," Gage told him as he smoothed the hair away from Forge's face. "Let's get through this mystery and make sure you're safe. Then we can make plans." Gage kissed him hard, tongue exploring, then gentled it and sat back up. "You should eat your lunch…." Gage's mouth fell open and he turned to Forge.

"What is it?" Forge asked.

"That thumb drive. The one we found in the safe. You had already taken the things back downstairs, so you put it in one of Granger's puzzle boxes for safekeeping. We never showed that to Coleridge."

Forge shrugged.

"I think we need to look at that once again." Gage had a faraway look. "Do you remember that blank file on the drive? Shit, what if there was something in that file and we couldn't see it."

Forge shook his head. "What do you mean?"

"White lettering on a white background. I never checked to see if there was anything there. I saw a blank screen and thought the file was blank. Granger said the password was in the safe. What if he hid it in plain sight on that drive?"

Forge sat up and picked up his spoon. "You could be right. After lunch, we'll go back to the house and get it."

"No," Gage said quickly. "I'll go get it after we eat. I'd like you to stay here and be safe. I'll phone ahead to make sure everything is all right. But Harv is needed elsewhere, so I've got to pull him off watching the house to start a new job. I won't do that until later this evening, though. There's a woman whose husband has been threatening her during their divorce. He's a bodybuilder, and unfortunately she claims he's taken too many steroids and is prone to fits of rage."

Forge frowned as he swirled his soup. "I've seen Harv. He's rather small. How is he going to stand up to some roid-raged ball of muscle?"

Gage's mouth turned up in an almost evil grin. "Harv can take care of himself, and it doesn't matter how big they are—if you break their knees, they fall hard. And Harv is a master at self-defense, as well as a number of martial arts. I've seen him take on a man almost three hundred pounds and leave him rolling on the ground in pain. So don't worry about him. Worry about the out-of-control bodybuilder. He's the one who's likely to end up in the hospital if he comes at Harv's client." Gage was still grinning, and Forge knitted

141

his brows together in order to try to figure it out. "Besides, I don't think I could keep Harv away from this client if I tried. She's the one who got away from him a number of years ago."

"You're kidding?"

"No." Gage grinned. "He still cares for her and asked for the assignment. Margie and I discussed it, and we thought it best. You'll be safe here until we're sure the threat has passed, and Harv has been busy installing an alarm system at your house."

"An alarm?"

"Yes. It's noninvasive and uses some of the latest technology. There are also cameras that you'll be able to access through the internet. We'll be able to watch the house from here and know if anything is amiss. It will be much more cost-effective than having someone physically watching the house day and night. And once this is over, you'll be safer there. The costs were part of the original protection contract I sent over and what you approved with your lawyer."

Forge realized he must have looked shocked. "I'm sorry. This just came as a surprise."

"The alarm system isn't going to replace me, and I'm still going to make sure you're safe. I'll just have some help." They ate in silence for a bit, the *tink* of the spoons on the dishes the only sound other than an occasional slurp. "I didn't mean to upset you."

"You didn't and you're right. It will be good to have an alarm so I'll know if someone else is there, especially when I'm home alone." Forge suspected that he'd be spending a lot of time at home alone.

"What are you afraid of? Really afraid of? Not the answer that you tell yourself or the one you think I want to hear, but the truth." Gage set down his spoon, turning to him.

Forge felt the depth of his gaze down to his soul. He set down the spoon, his appetite flying away. "I'm afraid of being alone. My parents are dead, both of them. Dad died last year, as I said before. My mother had a lot of emotional issues when I was young and was often under a doctor's care. I don't think I ever got over not actually having my mother for a lot of the time I was growing up. She passed away eleven years ago."

"Is that when you met Granger?"

"No. But losing my mom is when I think I decided that I wanted to stay with him. We'd been dating for a year or so, and it was at that point that he asked me to move in with him and to try to build a life together. I agreed, and we had a good life for a number of years." Forge sighed. "Sometimes it's hard to look at yourself and your motivations in a clear light. When you do, they seem too self-serving and shallow. I needed Granger back then…."

Gage nodded. "You didn't want to be alone, and he loved you. There's nothing wrong with wanting to be loved."

"But I chose him because he was easy, and what if I'm doing that again?" Forge didn't want to sound stupid, but he also didn't want to make the same mistakes he had in the past.

Gage laughed, out loud and hard, turning his face toward the ceiling. "I don't think that any of the guys I've dated will describe me as easy or low maintenance. I keep a schedule that would drive most people crazy. So I'm not uncomplicated or convenient, and you aren't making the same mistake all over. Don't forget that you and I spent years apart, and I don't want to do that again." He grew serious, looking over at Forge. "But if you don't feel the same way… you don't need to make up an excuse. When this case is over, we can go our separate ways, or just be friends, if that's what you'd like."

"That isn't what I want," Forge said quickly and much more forcefully than he expected to. "I don't want to be just friends, and I don't want to go our separate ways. But I keep wondering if things aren't moving too fast."

"How long have things been over between you and Granger?"

"Months… many months," Forge answered. "And I know I have the right to move on. But…." He groaned. "Everything is just so mixed up in my head. I thought things were settled with Granger, and then I find these notes and he seemed so contrite in them. I know that even if he hadn't been killed, we wouldn't have gotten back together. I guess I want this over so I can feel free again."

"Then give yourself the time and the chance to do that. If that's what you want. I waited seventeen years to find you again—I can wait a little longer for you to find your way." Gage leaned closer, resting his head on Forge's shoulder. "Don't wonder if I'm going to disappear. It's not going to happen."

Forge breathed a huge sigh of relief and picked up his spoon to finish the soup. Gage did the same a few moments later, and Forge missed the closeness of having Gage pressing right next to him. He liked that Gage felt he could lean on him, just like Forge knew he could lean on Gage.

Once they were done, Forge took care of the dishes, placing them in the sink of the kitchenette, and then returned to the living area.

"Please stay here. If you need to, you can check the monitors out at the front desk. I'm going to run to the house to get the box. I'll be back as soon as I can. I also want to check that the alarm system is working properly."

"But what if something happens?"

"Just stay here, and I'll message you if I need anything." Gage walked to where Forge sat. "I need to know that you're safe. So please stay here, and I'll be back as soon as I can." He leaned down to kiss him. "God, I love that I can do that whenever I want to." He slid his hand around the back of Forge's neck, his heat boring into Forge. Gage didn't move closer; he simply looked deeply into Forge's eyes as warmth and comfort spread through him. "I'll see you soon." Gage's hand slipped away, and he hesitated before turning and leaving the room.

Forge pulled his phone out of his pocket, placed it on the table, and listened as the doors closed. He might have heard the garage overhead door go up and down, but he wasn't sure. Forge did know it was dead quiet as he sat on the sofa, listening and waiting. He checked his watch. If Gage went right to the house and came right back, it would take less than an hour.

He thought of turning on the television, but was too restless to sit still for very long and ended up pacing the room, unsure why he was so nervous. Gage knew how to take care of himself, and he was only going to the house, which Harv had been keeping an eye on for him, so this shouldn't be too big a deal. Still, his nerves wouldn't settle down.

Forge jumped when his phone vibrated on the table. He yanked it to his ear, answering it with fumbling fingers.

"It's Harvey." He sounded breathless. "Someone set the house on fire. The fire department has been called, and Gage is on his way to pick you up. He said to be ready and he'll bring you back."

Forge went cold as his imagination took over, picturing flames shooting out of the windows. "Okay. I'll be waiting." He hung up and didn't know what he should do first. He sort of stopped and started, wondering what was going to be left of his home when he got there. Then he hurried through the office, closing the doors behind him, and stepped outside. His head spun, and he desperately needed some fresh air.

The sun shone brightly, but all Forge could think about was the house and what was happening. He hoped the damage wasn't too bad, but if someone had set a fire, then he had no illusions about what he was going to be walking into. It was going to be bad.

Forge closed the door and leaned against the building, watching the driveway for when Gage came back.

He knew his mistake as soon as a black car turned around the side of the building, then skidded to a stop. Forge turned back to the door, but strong arms encircled his waist, pulling him off his feet and into the back seat of the car. He was still kicking as the door slammed closed behind him, and they peeled out.

"You really thought you were going to be able to get the better of us?" a guy asked from the front seat.

Forge lifted his gaze as Stanley Lucci turned from the passenger seat to glare at him. Forge knew he was dead. He'd seen the boss's son and could ID him. This was kidnapping, and they were never going to let him get out of this alive.

CHAPTER 8

"*No!*" GAGE screamed from inside his car as he saw the black Mercedes pull out of the parking lot. He dialed Forge's number even as he whipped around when they passed. He hoped he was jumping to the wrong conclusion, but when the call went to voicemail, he knew exactly what had happened. Somehow they had gotten to Forge.

Gage put in another call. "Detective Coleridge, please. It's an emergency. I need him now. Someone is being kidnapped, and I need his help." That seemed to bypass the chain of command, and Coleridge came on the line in seconds. "It's Gage Livingston. Forge Reynolds has been taken. I'm following a black Mercedes down Brown Deer Road, heading toward the freeway." He gave the license number. "It's an Illinois plate."

"I have it. I'm putting out an APB right now, and I'll get squad cars. It's best if you don't follow."

"They've already seen me and are trying to lose me, but that isn't going to happen." Gage took a turn at dangerous speed and floored it, not letting them out of his sight. "I'll stay on the phone with you if you like."

"I need to get to my car. I'm going to put you through to dispatch. They'll stay with you. Explain to them what's going on. Hang on."

Gage got hold music through his car speakers as he made two more turns. These assholes were seriously reckless.

"This is dispatch," a man said, and Gage told him what was happening.

"I'm on Green Bay Road right now, heading south. We're going to pass Silver Spring at any second." Gage made another turn. "We're on Silver Spring now, heading toward the highway. God, I hope no one is in the way, because they're traveling like a bat out of hell."

"We have them at the freeway overpass. There are cars waiting for them there."

Gage didn't slow down when they turned onto a residential street before reaching the freeway. He relayed his position and was told that there were police cars up ahead. Gage certainly hoped so. He gripped the wheel as hard as he could and sped up, coming within a few feet of the back of the car. Sirens got closer, overlapping as they continued. Jesus, at this speed, if anyone was out and about, they were going to be in real trouble.

They came back onto Green Bay Road and took a turn, followed by yet another. "They're on a dead-end street," Gage relayed, and told them exactly where he was. Sirens converged and grew louder and louder.

The back passenger door opened, and Gage saw someone fall out and roll from the edge of the pavement onto the grass. He knew instantly it was Forge and screeched to a stop next to him, using the car to shield him from the other vehicle, which spun around with a loud squeal worthy of any action movie. Gage got down as the car sped past, expecting shots but hearing nothing except the roar of an engine as it zoomed by.

Sirens followed, and Gage gave his position as he grabbed his phone off the passenger seat and opened the door, transferring the call to the handset. "They're heading back toward Green Bay Road. I need an ambulance. They threw Forge out of the back seat." He reached Forge as Forge rolled over, groaning. "Don't move. I have help on the way." Gage kept talking. "We're in front of the stone ranch house with gray trim."

"We have an ambulance heading to your location, and Detective Coleridge is on his way as well. Other cars are pursuing the Mercedes."

"Okay. I'm going to put you on speaker and try to help Forge." He set the phone on the grass, put on the speaker, and bent over Forge. "Where does it hurt?"

"I knew it was you behind us, even though they didn't let me see out."

"Did you break anything?" Blood covered Forge's forehead. Gage raced to the car, opened the trunk, and pulled out his first aid kit. Sirens converged on his location as he got some gauze and found where Forge was bleeding.

"I don't think anything is broken. I rolled as soon as I hit the ground and tried not to stop myself." His military training had to have kicked in, thankfully. Most people would try to stop themselves and get hurt even worse.

Police cars and an ambulance pulled to a halt as people came out of the houses, looking around. Uniformed police officers kept them back while the EMTs and Coleridge approached.

Gage stood and stepped back, not wanting to leave Forge for a second, but needing to give the EMTs a chance to work.

"What the hell happened?" Detective Coleridge asked.

"They were cornered and needed to get away. I guess they figured if they dumped Forge, I'd stop and they could get out of the pickle they were in." Gage watched as the emergency personal transferred Forge to a backboard.

"I'm not injured that badly," Forge protested.

"Let them make sure of that," Gage said as gently as he could, kneeling down to take Forge's hand. He stroked it gently and turned to Coleridge. "He hasn't told me who took him. I was more concerned with making sure he was okay."

"Stanley Lucci. He was in the front seat. The other men were the ones from the party at your dad's," Forge said as they worked on him. "They were arguing about what they were doing. Stanley thought this was a great idea, but the guy in the back with me wasn't so happy and was sure Stanley's father was going to have a fit. He was scared, and he was the one who dumped me out of the car."

"You're going to be all right, and Coleridge is going to make sure they don't get away." Gage turned to Coleridge, who was on the phone, smiling.

"Excellent. I want to talk to the arresting officer as soon as he's available. We have some serious charges to level, including kidnapping. Yes, we have a credible witness, and he isn't getting off. He may be able to pay his way out in Illinois, but he isn't doing that here." Coleridge hung up. "The state police have him in custody. They stopped him on the freeway, and they tried to talk their way out of the jam they're in."

"Where are they?"

"Being transported to county lockup. The charges will be presented downtown, and since we're leveling kidnapping, it's likely the state prosecutor will take them on. That's good, because they're less likely than some of the local folks to be in daddy Lucci's pocket." Coleridge seemed pleased, and Gage turned back to Forge, who was looking better now that the bleeding had stopped and he was cleaned up.

"Are you in any pain?" an EMT asked.

"My hands are sore from the scrapes, as are my knees, but other than that, I'm fine. Do I need stitches in my head?"

"I don't believe so. The bleeding has stopped, and we've been able to clean you up. You're also moving your head, legs, and feet without any issues."

"Yes, and my back and neck don't hurt. I was in the Army. They taught us how to roll and land, so that's what I did." Forge moved his arms and legs and then sat up once they removed him from the board. "I'm really fine." He shook hands with both the EMTs. "But I want to thank you for your help."

"You were very lucky," the lead EMT said.

"I know." Forge looked at Gage, and warmth spread through Gage. He knelt and leaned forward to hug Forge as hard as he dared.

"Don't you dare do that again. I don't think my heart stopped pounding for a second. I stayed behind them like glue because there

was no way anyone was going to take you away from me again."
Gage clamped his eyes closed as relief and love raced through him.
Tears ran down his cheeks, and he was man enough to let them
fall. Forge held his heart, and Gage had felt fear like he'd never
experienced before, not even when he wasn't able to move his
arms and legs.

"I didn't mean to," Forge said, holding him in return.

"How did they get you?"

"Harvey called and said the house was on fire," Forge said,
and Gage shook his head. "He said that you were on your way over
to get me."

"Harv would never have called you, and he certainly never
would have said his name was Harvey. He hasn't gone by that in
years." Gage breathed deeply, relieved at how narrowly they'd
avoided disaster. "And the house is fine, or at least it was when I
left it and Harv. I hurried back with what I went after and happened
to see them pulling away, and I knew something was wrong."

Forge held him tighter. "I knew I'd been set up as soon as
they turned the corner."

"At least you're okay." Gage released Forge and helped him
stand.

Forge gasped and breathed deeply.

"Are you dizzy?" one EMT asked.

"No. I'm fine. Just relieved that I'm in one piece. I really
thought I was gone. I'd seen the men who took me before, and
I didn't think they were going to let me go alive." He turned to
Coleridge. "They know I've seen them."

Coleridge nodded and stepped closer. "When they pulled the
car over, one of the men, the one in the back seat… he wasn't doing
so well. They think he was pistol-whipped, most likely by Stanley,
and it's likely that was for getting rid of you."

Forge nodded. "He didn't want to be part of it, and I think he
panicked and pushed me out, hoping they could all get away, especially
if Gage stayed behind to help me. It's the only thing that makes sense."

He shook violently once from head to toe. "Can I go home now? Or do you need pictures of what happened to me for evidence?"

Detective Coleridge had one of the officers take photographs, and he got a statement from each of them before backing away.

"Detective," Gage said. "Stop by the house tomorrow, and we'll be able to answer any additional questions you have." He had every intention of taking Forge back to his office so he could rest. He guided Forge to his car and helped him get inside.

"They knew where I was," Forge said. "They faked a call from Harv to get me to come outside."

"I know. It seems they were watching us a lot more closely than I realized. But you're safe now, thank God." Gage felt like an idiot. He should have taken Forge with him. At least then he could have kept him close. "I should have been—"

"Stop that," Forge told him sharply. "I should have called you to verify where you were instead of getting upset and racing outside. They couldn't have gotten in, so they had to lure me out, and they did it very easily." He turned to watch out the side window. "In fact, I fell for it like a sucker. I should have stayed put. If there was something wrong, you would have called me, not had someone else do it. That I should have known. You didn't put me in danger—I did that myself."

"Hey. Stop it." Gage pulled to the side of the road. "You're safe, and beating ourselves or each other up for what could have happened isn't going to get us anywhere." Personally, Gage felt like a complete fool. He should have known how closely they were being observed. "I wonder how they found out about Harv?"

"All they had to do was listen to us talking at the house somehow. Harv did scare the shit out of those guys who were hanging around. I bet they figured out he was there and used that information when they needed to." Forge continued watching out the windows, then lowered his mirror. "I don't see anyone behind us."

Gage stifled a groan. He sure as hell hoped this was over, at least for the moment. Stanley's family had worse problems now than them. Stanley wasn't going to tell anyone anything, Gage was sure of that, and though his lawyers might not be able to get him off, he wasn't going to sell out the family business. Gage shook his head, trying to think of what their next move should be.

"I want to go back to my house. I need to sleep in my own bed. Besides, they know about your office, and while it's safer there, it isn't doing us any real good." Forge drummed his fingers on the armrest. "I'm just so tired of running and being scared. It really sucks."

"I know it does." Gage continued on the same course and headed for the office anyway. "We'll spend the night at the office because it's safer and has more surveillance, and go to the house in the morning to meet Coleridge," he said, hoping he was making the right decision. "The puzzle box with the drive in it is under your seat. I think I remembered the right one."

"It should be the only one with something inside that would rattle."

"Then I got the right one." Gage smiled, and they finished the drive in silence. Once they pulled into the office garage, they got out and went upstairs together, Gage holding Forge's hand. He checked that all the security was working, which it was, and then they went in to the living area and placed everything they had on the table.

Forge opened the box and handed Gage the drive they'd found in the safe. Gage inserted it into his computer and located the empty file. He opened it and highlighted the file to make any text appear. There was nothing.

"Dammit. I was so hopeful."

Forge stared at the blank screen too. "So was I. There wasn't anything in the safe. We've gone over it more than once. We even checked all the coin cases to make sure there wasn't anything inside and turned everything else upside down." He sat back and closed his eyes. "I'm so tired of all this."

"I know you are. But you're the only one who knew Granger well enough to figure this out. He loved puzzles, so how would he hide that password? He said it was there, and we have to assume, at least until we have nothing else to go on, that it's still there and he didn't remove it. Granger knew he was in danger or he wouldn't have left the note in the jade box." An idea popped into Gage's head. "Do you know which cloud storage service Granger used?"

"I think it was the Microsoft one," Forge said with a heavy sigh.

Gage had intended to bring up the interface, but what good was it going to do? "Let me make you something to eat and you can lie down for a while." It was going on dinnertime, and they had had so much excitement. Gage was starving, and Forge had to be hungry as well.

"Okay," Forge said, with no energy at all.

Gage put aside what he was thinking and scooted closer to Forge. The mystery would still be there in a few hours. Forge needed some comfort now, and that was so much more important. He gathered Forge to him, and they sat quietly with Gage holding him tightly. Forge trembled in his arms more than once.

"I honestly thought they were going to kill me. I saw who they were, and there was no going back from that. I can testify as to what they did."

Gage knew just how lucky they were that the man in the back seat got scared and pushed Forge out of the car. Forge was lucky to be alive, and Gage quietly beat himself up for putting Forge in danger. He thought he'd done the right thing, that Forge would be safer here than with him. Plans should have been made to… he should have been better prepared. Instead, he'd made a mistake that had resulted in… he'd nearly lost Forge. Gage buried his face in Forge's hair as his thoughts came in ragged spurts and fragments. Maybe he was too close to this job. Lord knows he was too close to Forge. Maybe it was impairing his judgment.

"It's all right," Forge said softly. "You can stop muttering under your breath. I know what you're doing, and you need to stop."

"But I almost lost you." The fear he'd felt in the car reared up again, this time more severely, threatening to overwhelm him.

Gage quivered and closed his eyes to try to regain his composure. "I lost you for seventeen years, and then I almost had you for less than a week because I wasn't good enough to protect you."

"I was the one who fell for their trick, not you. If anything I put myself in danger because I didn't listen to you. I was safe here. Even with them out here, they couldn't get inside to me, and you were on your way back already. I'd have been fine if I'd have stayed where I was. Instead, I let someone I didn't know scare me."

"You thought it was Harv."

"But it wasn't, and if I'd have been thinking clearly, I'd have known it wasn't him and would have been just fine. So stop beating yourself up." Forge held him closer, and slowly some of the tension and recrimination racing through his mind settled down. "None of us is superhuman."

"No, we aren't." Gage sighed and wished to hell he *had* been superhuman. Then Forge wouldn't have been kidnapped and they would have a clearer picture of what exactly was going on. He nodded and slowly stood to go make them something to eat.

Forge sat back and reached for his phone. "I need to talk to Granger's parents." He dialed the number, and Gage left the room to allow Forge to talk in peace.

In the kitchenette, he found Margie had made sure the refrigerator was stocked, and got out the things to make BLTs. Whenever he was stressed and needed comfort food, that was what he wanted. He used the microwave to cook the bacon, cut up a tomato, broke the lettuce leaves, and started making toast. Gage listened but didn't hear any shouting or arguing, so he hoped things were going as well as could be expected with Granger's parents.

"I don't think so," Forge said rather loudly, and Gage realized he'd jumped the gun. "I'm sorry about all that's happened, but Granger's will is still in effect and that's all there is to it."

Gage peered around the corner to where Forge stood in front of the sofa.

"He did what?" Forge glanced his way and then began pacing. "No. That isn't going to happen, and I'm sorry to have to say this, but unless you have a newer will…."

Gage set the knife aside and took the finished bread out of the toaster, then put in some more before standing next to Forge.

"I see. So you were only assuming. But it seems Granger didn't update his will, so everything will come to me, including his partnership in the law firm, which I have already spoken to Francis about. He's well aware of my position."

Gage put his hand on Forge's shoulder just to let him know he was there to back him up.

"I understand what that meant to Granger. Francis is trying to get me to settle quickly, typical lawyer, so he can get the share in the partnership cheaply. But that isn't what's going to happen. We'll see it through the end of the fiscal year and then go from there…." Forge began pacing again. "No. I intend to split the proceeds of the sale of Granger's partnership with you. It was his life's work and I won't cut you out of that. But I'll do what I think is best, and you're going to have to leave it at that for now. I don't want to make any quick decisions at this point." Forge relaxed, and Gage assumed the tone of the conversation had eased. "Yes… I've instructed them to release the body directly to you. Tell me what arrangements you've made and I'll come down." Sweat broke out on Forge's forehead. He listened for a few more minutes and then said a very quiet goodbye, ending the call with tears running down his cheeks.

"I take it the call didn't go well."

Forge shook his head. "Francis called them about Granger's partnership. He seemed to think that since we were in the process of separating, Granger probably had a more up-to-date will, which he couldn't find and they don't have, or that they should put pressure on me to sell him Granger's portion of the partnership. He didn't say it outright, but they got the impression that Francis would make it worth their while to get me to sell right away." Forge turned and fell into Gage's embrace. "They used to be like my parents, and now

I don't know…. The last few months have been hard for them too. Believe it or not, I know they did their best to try not to take sides, and they gave Granger hell for his affair." Forge held him tighter.

"You know, they're Granger's parents, and when push comes to shove, blood is thicker than water."

"I know. It just seems like I've lost so much in a short period of time. A year ago my life was so good. Granger and I had a relatively happy life, his family was my family… we… damn…."

Gage held him and said nothing, letting Forge work through whatever he felt he needed to.

"It was all just a fucking illusion. I try to think back to happier times, and all I see now is the lead-up to the two of us falling apart and Granger's affair. What I thought was solid was really just sand, with our lives built on it."

"No, it wasn't. Things change—people change. Would the Granger you fell in love with allow people like Stanley Lucci and his family into your lives? I somehow doubt it. Granger changed, and as the years passed, you did too. What you both wanted grew along different paths. It happens."

"But what if that happens to us?" Forge asked. "Or am I jumping ahead?"

"It won't happen to us. It can't." Gage took Forge's hand and placed it on his chest. "I feel you right here, and I always have. I carried the young man who sat next to my hospital bed in my heart for years, and now he's grown up… into you. That space inside… it's all yours and it always has been. So as we get older and slow down, you'll still be there. Maybe the passion will cool between us, but the heat will still burn. I expect things to change—maybe Granger expected you to stay the same. I don't know. But you can't beat yourself up over it."

Forge lifted his head to meet Gage's gaze. "It isn't that. It's like the life I thought I built was an illusion. How can I trust my judgment after that?"

"You want head answers to heart questions," Gage said softly. "And you'll never get anywhere like that. Stop trying to think your way through everything and let yourself feel it. Your heart will tell you what it wants. Mine has been speaking loud and clear for days, and it's never wrong. I bet yours isn't either." Gage raised his eyebrows and continued holding Forge until their stomachs rumbled in near unison.

"Okay. I guess that's enough wallowing in self-pity for today," Forge pronounced. Gage rolled his eyes. "Okay, it's enough for the year."

"Now that's the Forge I remember. Never let anything get you down for long." Gage patted Forge's leg and stood to return to the kitchen to finish dinner.

GAGE BROUGHT in a tray with two plates and a pile of sandwiches— he'd cooked the entire pound of bacon—glasses of iced tea, and tons of napkins, setting it on the coffee table.

"Are you feeding an army?" Forge teased as Gage set out plates and passed out the initial sandwiches, which didn't last very long. They were obviously hungry and devoured two each before slowing down. "Okay, I take that back. You were feeding an army of two." Forge drank some tea and set his glass down.

"Are you done?"

"Just resting," Forge told him, then reached for a third BLT once Gage did. "You know, this is going to blow my diet for weeks." Forge ate the sandwich with just as much gusto, although more slowly this time. "God, those are good. It's been a long time since I had one. Granger—" Forge stopped midsentence. "They weren't his thing."

"He didn't like BLT sandwiches? Why on earth did you ever date him? These are like the comfort food of the gods. There's mayo and tomato, crispy lettuce, and bacon—lots of bacon—and I subscribe to the 'everything feels better after bacon' philosophy of life." Gage waved his arms dramatically, and Forge leaned back in his seat, laughing deeply. "There must have been something wrong with him. It's *bacon*." Gage waved his hands to make his point, sending Forge into another fit of laughter.

"What about vegetarians?" Forge teased.

"I understand they have tofu bacon. I don't know how it tastes. But let's see. There's turkey bacon and veggie bacon… why? Because everyone loves bacon. It's one of the basic food groups: milk, meat, fruit and veg, grains, and bacon, lots and lots of bacon." Gage couldn't hold it in any longer, laughing right along with Forge. He liked that he could be ridiculously silly with Forge.

As the laughter wore down, Gage lay back, his head against the sofa cushions, staring up at the ceiling. "Jesus Christ!" He groaned and sat up straight, a light coming on. "Why in the hell didn't I think of it before?"

"What?" Forge asked.

"The password. It was in front of our faces all along. We were looking inside the file, but what if it was simpler than that? What if the password was the name of the file?" He jumped to his feet and raced to his bag for his computer. Gage pulled it out and hurried back to the table. He opened the laptop and signed in. "Okay. Let's try OneDrive and see if this works." Gage brought up the sign-in page, and Forge told him the email address to use. Then he grabbed the jump drive and entered the name of the file, Granger&Forge, just the way Granger had saved it. He pressed enter and got a message that the account or password was incorrect or invalid. Gage tried again to no avail. "Maybe it's iCloud."

Forge shook his head. "Granger didn't use Apple products. Not even an iPhone. He didn't like them." He help up his iPhone with a grin. "I thought he was crazy, but that was his opinion."

"Then we could try Dropbox." Gage brought up the application login and entered the email address and password. There weren't many cloud options left. Gage crossed his fingers and pressed enter. The screen went white and then the computer indicated it was working. Then the Dropbox main screen came up with all the stored file systems listed, right there in front of him. "We're in."

"Holy cow," Forge said.

"Yes. Holy cow is right." There were a lot of files and directories. "It's going to take a while to go through all of this."

"What are you going to do?" Forge asked as the application asked if he wanted to install the agent on his computer. Gage clicked yes, and after a fast install, he began downloading the files. There were thousands of them. "Are these his client files? I don't want to compromise anything."

"No. These are all about the Lucci family. Look at how they're organized. He must have gathered information on them for a long time." Gage whistled. "God, if he were alive, they'd probably disbar him for breach of fiduciary duty, or as an agent of the court knowing about criminal activity and not reporting it. Where in the hell did he get all this?" Gage was just looking at the file names and organization, and the amount boggled the mind. He sat back as meg after meg of information came down to the computer, as file system after file system populated.

"Holy shit," Forge said, pointing to a set of files. "Open those."

Gage complied, and Forge lifted the computer onto his lap. "Don't move or delete anything," Gage warned.

"I won't," Forge said breathlessly as he opened and looked through document after document. "Son of a bitch! The Luccis weren't Granger's clients—they were Francis's! He brought them into the firm." Forge turned the screen so Gage could see it better, and sure enough, there were copies of client engagement files, signed by Stanley Lucci and Francis Peterborough. "That bastard."

Gage let Forge look through the files, Forge getting redder and angrier by the second. "That bastard," Forge repeated… again and again.

"What?"

"That *bastard*!" Forge nearly yelled. "I thought Granger had gotten mixed up with these people, but it was Francis. Granger was collecting data on them to try to protect himself. All these documents have Francis as the author." Forge shook with rage. "This was all that asshole's fault. Shit."

"Okay." Gage took the computer back. "Let's not jump to any conclusions."

"To hell with that! I'm going to jump to a bunch of conclusions here. Francis took on the Lucci family as clients, and Granger got wind of what they were doing. He gathered the information and saved it off. My guess is he wouldn't go to the police because of his jurist ethics and beliefs, but he saved the information in case something happened to him."

Gage sighed. "That's one way of looking at it. But we don't know yet. There's a lot to go through."

Forge nodded. "Then we'd better get started. Because I'm going to spit-roast Francis when I get my hands on him, and so not in the good way." He stood, pacing, muttering under his breath, and occasionally throwing an air punch while Gage continued going through the information.

"We have to call Coleridge," Gage said. "There's too much here for us to keep this to ourselves. He needs to have this to turn over to federal authorities. It will bring down the entire family organization."

"But what about Francis? Do you think he had Granger killed?" Forge asked. "I thought it was the Luccis because he knew too much, but I bet Francis had it done because he realized Granger might be gathering information. Which was stupid."

Forge was on a tear, and Gage figured it was best to let him run himself out. He continued going through the files and had to admit, it didn't look particularly good for Francis or the Luccis. Granger had a ton on all of them, and it was a sure bet that once all this got out, there would be investigations—and God knew what would come of it all.

"Look at this." Gage turned the computer.

Forge stopped pacing and came over. "What am I looking at?"

"A confidential memo from Granger to Francis." Gage gave Forge time to read it. "Looks like Granger wasn't happy about the clients Francis was bringing in and was worried it would damage the firm."

"Damage it? This is going to kill it. There will be no firm once this comes out." Forge sat back as though he'd been beaten. "All of Granger's hard work will evaporate like fog in the sun. He was trying to save the firm and pressure Francis to drop them as clients so they could move forward."

"You don't drop people like the Luccis. Once they're in the door, they don't leave the party willingly." This was really bad. Gage grabbed his phone and sent a text to his father. He received an immediate answer that his father and his mother were having a fine time. Then, with a sigh, he phoned Coleridge. This couldn't wait until morning. Gage had to go through a number of people to get to Coleridge, but he was persistent.

"I'm sorry to bother you this late, but Forge and I figured out how to access Granger's files."

"How?" Coleridge asked with avid interest. Gage gave him the passcode they'd used. "Okay. Hold on." Coleridge put down the phone, and Gage heard him on a different call to someone else. Then he came back. "That seemed to be the phrase to decrypt the files on the laptop as well."

"Then you have access to what we have," Gage said with relief.

"It appears so. I'm on my way in to see what we have. I'll meet you and Forge at the house tomorrow as planned so we can discuss next steps."

"Very good. We'll see you then." Gage hung up and felt somewhat better. The police had the files and the information that Granger had collected. There was nothing else they could do now.

"What did he say?" Forge asked with a jittery tone in his voice.

"That he'll see us in the morning. They decrypted the laptop, and he's on his way in to examine the files." Gage returned to his computer and verified that all the files had been downloaded. Then

162

he paused the synching and separated from the application to make his copies of the files independent.

"What are you doing?"

"Just an insurance policy. I don't know how far the reach of the Lucci family extends, but once they find out this information exists and the police have it, they are going to try their best to make it disappear. But this copy is separate now. They could delete the master files and these will still remain."

"You don't trust Coleridge?"

"I do. He's a good man. But I don't trust everyone in the department. It only takes one person with access to wipe out everything." Gage felt better now that he had secure copies, but he went further and transferred the files to an encrypted jump drive, making sure Forge knew the passcode. "There isn't anything more we can do tonight. The police have the information, and now we have to give them a chance to do their jobs."

Forge nodded, sitting back once again. "This is never going to end. They'll arrest people, and then there will be trials and God knows what. I'm never going to be safe and be able to go back to…." Forge leaned forward, his head in his hands. "I wasn't expecting my life to be the way it's been. Granger is always going to be dead and… well… I found you again." Forge blindly reached out, and Gage took his hand. "My life was going to be different, but I'd hoped that it would settle down to where we could have a quiet life. Well, reasonably quiet anyway."

"Is that what you really want?" Gage tugged Forge to his feet and into his embrace. "Do you want to go back to the same quiet life you had with Granger? Because life with me won't be like that. You've seen the hours I work and what I do. I don't go into an office, unless it's this one, and I usually don't spend a lot of time here." Gage lifted Forge's chin slightly. "I want you in my life. I want to go to sleep next to you, and wake up in the morning and make love to you, for the rest of my life. If you asked me to, I'd shut down the agency and try to find a different job." Gage held his breath, waiting for Forge's answer. This would tell a lot about whether they could have a practical life together.

"No," Forge whispered. "I don't want you to do that."

"Then you have to know that if we're together, then things will change, for both of us. My clients hire me to protect them from people who want to hurt them, and by extension they'll want to get to me. The easiest way to do that is going to be through you." A chill raced up Gage's spine. "I don't want that to happen."

Forge rolled his eyes in that patented way he had whenever Gage said something he thought was stupid. "I can take care of myself. I'm not helpless and I'm not scared. I'm not going to live my life alone because I'm afraid of what might happen." He put his forehead against Gage's. "God, I want you in my life, and I'll do anything to have you. If that means I have to be on guard and vigilant, then I will." Forge blinked rapidly. "I can't be without you. I was sitting in the back seat of that damn car today, wondering if I was going to live, and all I could think was that I wasn't going to see you again, hold you, be able to roll over at night and curl up to you when things got cold or hard or frightening. And I was scared to death." He shook, and Gage closed his eyes, unable to bear the fear he saw welling in Forge's—fear that shouldn't be there if he'd have been doing his job.

"Forge, I—"

"Stop feeling guilty. There will be plenty of time for me to be scared, and I'm sure I'll relive what happened in my dreams." Forge pulled him closer, and damned if Gage didn't get hard in an instant when Forge's gaze bored deeply into his. "I want to forget. I want you to make me feel alive and wanted… I want…."

Gage didn't need to be told twice. He kissed Forge hard, holding him as tightly as he could. "I thought I was going to lose you forever." He backed Forge away from the table and toward the bedroom. They fumbled together, both wanting the same thing and neither willing to let go long enough to make it to the other room. Gage bumped into the doorframe, but he didn't care for an instant.

All that mattered was Forge's lips on his and the way Forge's hands, those amazing hands, worked their way under his shirt.

They reached the bed, falling onto it. Gage ended up under Forge's weight, and he loved it, holding him, continuing to kiss while trying his best to get rid of the clothes between them.

"Dammit," Forge gasped, and Gage sat up. His shirt wasn't going to survive if he didn't help. Forge's frustration was palpable, his hands shaking.

Gage rolled Forge onto his back and stood at the foot of the bed, shedding his clothes and divesting Forge of his. "You take my breath away." Forge lay naked and exposed to Gage's heated gaze. He swallowed and licked his lips to keep from drooling at the sight.

"I'm old...."

"You're beautiful and you always will be." Gage leaned over Forge to prowl up the bed until their lips were inches apart. "You will always be the man who sat next to me in the hospital all those days, and the one who came to me before we were separated and gave me the night of passion I've never been able to forget." Gage circled one of Forge's nipples with his thumb, loving the quiver that went through Forge with the simplest touch—his touch. A shiver went through him at the way Forge responded to him.

"I remember that night too." Forge drew him closer. "I know you weren't very strong at that point, but you were all the man I could ever want then, and you still are now." He pulled Gage into a kiss and down on top of him, wrapping his legs around Gage's waist. "I want you to repeat what you did that night. Make me feel that same way."

Gage pulled Forge as tight to him as possible, cradling his back and head in his arms. "You were a dream come true when I saw you again." He knew he sounded corny, but it was how he felt. Seventeen years of hoping and dreaming, living in the past, were over. He had the man he'd always wanted.

"Then make me yours." Forge arched his back as Gage ran his hands down the silky smoothness of Forge's sides and over his hips to his hard butt. He continued deeper, teasing Forge's skin, running his fingers down the cleft as Forge shook under him.

"I waited for you for years, so I know you're wound up, but I want to take my time." Gage captured Forge's lips. "I'm going to drive you crazy." He skimmed his fingers over the tender flesh of Forge's opening. "I'm going to drive you wild until your eyes roll back in your head, and once you can't stand it anymore and you think you're going to fly apart, then and only then am I going to slide inside you and take you all the way to heaven. I love you, Forge Reynolds, I have for years, but I love you even more now, because you're right here. The memory of you was precious. The reality of you, with me right now, is completely divine, and I will do anything to make you happy."

And Gage did just that, eliciting a chorus of groans, whines, and whimpers that filled the room and grew louder and more urgent as he used his tongue and mouth on continually more sensitive areas. Forge shook like a leaf, making the entire bed vibrate, and damned if that wasn't as hot as the pleading for Gage to either stop or give him just a little more.

"Keeping me on the edge is mean…."

"No. It's beautiful." And it was. Forge's eyes were dark blue, edging toward black. "Your skin flushed, eyes wide and dark, your mouth hanging open. And your hands—you don't know what to do with your hands." Damn, the man had amazing hands, and he'd been using them, desperately, to try to pull away Gage's control. It hadn't worked up until now. Gage's own control was near the breaking point. He spread Forge's saliva-slicked thighs, exposing him, wet skin glistening in the light spilling in from the other room. Forge damn near sparkled with sweat, and his rich musky aroma hung in the air like the world's most amazingly intoxicating perfume. Gage hurriedly slicked himself and slid into Forge, slowly, steadily, to high-pitched calls for more.

When he reached bottom, Forge thumped him on the chest. "Don't you dare fucking stop."

"I wasn't…."

Forge did it again. "I'm just saying, you stop now and so help me I'll…." A groan, long, low, and toe-curling, sang through the room as Gage pulled out, then slammed back into Forge. "Yes… fuck me like you've been denied for seventeen years."

Something snapped in Gage's brain and he let go, giving in to passion, love, and everything else that made life worth living. Forge was his to love, to possess, and to make happy, just like he was Forge's. Sweat beaded off Gage, running down his chest and his forehead into his eyes. "I'll love on you forever."

"Just don't stop," Forge gritted between breaths, stroking himself and tensing more and more with each movement. Gage couldn't hold back for much longer but was determined to see Forge tumble before he allowed himself to come. Seconds later Forge arched his back, crying out loudly and deeply, coming as Gage lost his last bit of control, spilling deep inside Forge.

He didn't dare move. Gage slowly came back to awareness and hoped to hell he hadn't hurt Forge when he'd lost it. However, judging by the smile on his face, Forge was just as happy as Gage, and he tugged Gage down into a sweet kiss that soothed away his worries. "I know you'll never hurt me."

"But I was too rough—"

"Nope, you were perfect." Forge gathered him into his arms, and Gage lay still, cradled in an embrace of love he'd never expected to find again, but would fight with everything he had to protect.

CHAPTER 9

FORGE WOKE, after the best night's sleep he'd had in months, to Gage rolling over, pulling him closer, and pressing his hard cock insistently against Forge's ass. "You're insatiable," Forge teased as he flexed his butt.

"Only for you," Gage muttered. "Are you sore?"

"A little." Forge grinned, feeling cheeky. "I could definitely go for another round, but we're supposed to meet Coleridge in half an hour. And if I'm not mistaken, Margie is out in her office. Now, you might want to show off your prowess…."

"Oh God, no." Gage pulled the pillow over his face. "That can't happen," he said, voice muffled. "I'll never hear the end of it."

"The end of what?" Forge asked innocently.

"She'll say 'I told you so' to me every day for the rest of my life. She's been hounding me for years to find someone and…."

"Well, you just tell her you were picky and had to wait for perfection." Forge smiled as beatifically as he could, and Gage grabbed him. Forge squealed like a girl until he got hold of himself, kissed Gage, then squirmed out of his grasp. "Come on. Let's get dressed." Forge got out of the bed and hurried to the bathroom. He cleaned up quickly and went back to dress so they wouldn't be late. Gage was still in bed, so Forge pulled away the covers and smacked him on his butt. "Dang. Now you laze in bed." Forge was excited to put all this behind them and move on. The sooner they talked with Coleridge and got him whatever he needed, the better off they were going to be. "Get up, or I'll…." He leaned forward to lightly bite Gage on the buttcheek.

"Did you turn carnivorous?" Gage fake groused as he rolled over. "No biting anything else." He put his hands over his dick, stood, and hurried out of the room.

Forge giggled, watching Gage's marked ass disappear behind the bathroom door. "We have to leave in five minutes." He left the room and gathered the things they'd brought from the house, including the box and the original jump drive. "Do you want to bring your computer?" Forge called back once he heard Gage in the bedroom area.

"No. Leave it here. I'll put the spare drive in the locked files, and we'll see what happens. I'm keeping what we have as security, and we'll let it be known that if anything happens to us, the files will be sent to the media. That will keep everyone honest." Gage leaned around the doorframe, grinning as he flashed Forge a glimpse of chest before disappearing once again.

Forge finished getting things together and decided to leave the jade box where it was. There was no need to carry something that valuable along with them. "Are you ready?"

Gage appeared in jeans and a plain red T-shirt, looking delicious even in simple clothes. "Let's go." He led him out of the living quarters and into the office area, where Margie smiled, waving as they passed, as she talked on the phone.

"Good luck," she said softly, and Forge nodded as they hurried on through to the car to get into the passenger seat. He was nervous and excited, his leg bouncing while he waited for Gage.

It wasn't long before they were on their way, and he grew more and more anxious the closer they got to the house he'd shared with Granger. It was funny, but it didn't feel like home any longer. Forge wasn't sure where home was, but that house and what it represented, combined with what had happened there, made it not feel like his home anymore.

"I know you're nervous."

"Excited."

"Okay, excited." Gage smiled at him. "Just relax and we can get this over with." He turned into the driveway, where three cars were waiting for them. Forge crouched low and turned to Gage. "It's all right. Coleridge is getting out."

Forge relaxed and opened his door.

"I'll open the house," Gage offered, and Forge handed him his keys. Gage went to unlock the door while Forge met Coleridge and shook his hand.

"Who is with you?"

"Let's go inside and we'll talk," Coleridge said.

Forge tensed and eyed the car, ready to get back inside in case they'd judged him incorrectly. After all that had happened, he was jumpy as hell.

"It's all right. They're additional authorities." Detective Coleridge motioned to the door, and Forge entered his own home, still nervous and wondering what was going to happen next. All three men followed him, then closed the door behind them. "This is Agent Shepherd with the FBI here in Milwaukee, and this is Agent Martinez with the Chicago FBI."

"You've done us a huge service," Agent Martinez said, shaking his hand. "Our office has been investigating the Lucci family for years, but we haven't been able to get anything concrete on them, and then you uncover the holy grail of information hauls."

"What are you doing with it?" Forge asked, moving into the living room.

"We've had teams of people up all night analyzing what was in the files and figuring out who we could charge with what. So far our list is huge and getting bigger. We're going to take out the heart of the entire Lucci organization. Arrest warrants are being issued as we speak, and teams of agents are flying in to execute them. We aren't going to let anyone escape our net. Agent Shepherd here is in charge of rounding up the players in the Milwaukee area, and we have teams in St. Louis and other cities."

"Is one of the people being arrested Francis Peterborough?" Forge asked.

"I can't confirm any specific people at this time," Agent Shepherd said.

"Oh, you can't?" Forge was pissed at the agent's attitude. "Then maybe I'll see to it that copies of all the files are sent to the news media." He pulled out his phone. "All it will take is a phone call, and it hits the internet." His temper was on a very short leash. "Hell, a text will do it."

"You don't want to do that," Coleridge said.

"The files are mine. I inherited them from Granger, and as my property, I am free to do with them what I wish. The FBI or the government does not own them." Forge put his foot down, insisting they were going to play it his way.

"What do you want, Mr. Reynolds?" Agent Martinez asked coolly.

"First, did Stanley or his men kill Granger?" Forge looked for any prevarication.

Agent Martinez nodded. "We believe so, yes. He was trying to get possession of the information you gave to us. We're building the case with Detective Coleridge, but it's looking strong."

That was a relief. At least Granger could rest easily. His killer would be brought to justice. "Is Francis going to be arrested?" Forge asked again, taking Gage's hand. The confidence he'd had a few moments earlier began to fade.

The agents exchanged glances. "Yes, he is," Agent Shepherd answered.

"Good. I want to be there when you do it. And just so you know, I've been kidnapped, chased, threatened, eavesdropped on, followed, scared, nervous, frightened, and wondering if I was going to be killed… all in the last few days. So, believe me, after that, I'll take on the entire US government to get what I want." He squeezed Gage's hand, and the agents conferred.

"You know this is very irregular."

"Yes. But I want to be there, and I want you to do it in the office in front of everyone. I want humiliation. I can even help you make sure he's there. I'll send him a message to say that I'm willing to sell him Granger's share of the firm. He'd wet himself in front of a jury for that." They were not going to tell Forge no. This was the one thing that was nonnegotiable.

"All right. But we'll assign you an agent that you must stay with the entire time."

Forge thanked Agent Shepherd and sat down with Gage next to him. He folded his arms over his chest. "When do we leave?"

"JUST LET them take the lead and do what they say," Gage told him as he drove downtown, following Agent Shepherd's car.

"I will." Forge smiled as they parked in the garage of the building of Granger's law firm, met the agents, and rode up in the elevator. "Francis should be here now."

Agent Shepherd nodded. "Do you believe he'll come meet you?"

"Most likely he'll be waiting for me in his office." The doors slid open, and Forge exited with Gage and walked right up to the receptionist. "Francis is expecting us." He continued to Francis's office door. He opened it, poked his head inside to make sure Francis was in his office, and then stood back to let the agents in.

"What the hell is this?" Francis asked loud enough to alert the entire office, which was delicious.

"Mr. Peterborough, you're under arrest." Agent Shepard read the whole list of charges off, then read Francis his rights as Francis sputtered the entire time.

"Do you know who I am?" he asked indignantly just before Forge heard the clink of handcuffs. Now *that* was a gorgeous sound.

"Yeah, I know who you are," Forge said quietly as he peered through the doorway at Francis. "A mob lawyer who's going up the river." He tried not to giggle out loud as agents swarmed the office with a series of warrants, ordering everyone around. It was a beautiful sight, though Forge was glad Granger wasn't around to see it. The death of his legal practice was something that might have killed him. Granger had put his lifeblood into this place, and now it was sinking faster than the Titanic.

"You can come in," Agent Shepherd said. "You have two minutes, and then we'll take him away."

Forge nodded, squeezing Gage's hand, and entered the office. Two men stood on either side of Francis, who was dressed in one of his expensive suits. His hands were behind his back, and he glared at Forge with more hatred than he'd ever seen in his life before spitting out, "I hope you know what you've done to this firm, to Granger's life's work."

Forge walked up to Francis, backhanded him on the left cheek, and then used the other hand to backhand him again. "I didn't do anything. That was all you and everyone knows it. Granger didn't let slime into his law practice. You did. His mistake was trusting a jackass like you. Well, you're done." He clenched his fists, wanting to smack Francis again.

"You saw him—that was assault," Francis threatened.

"These good gentlemen didn't see a thing," Forge said with a smile. "And just so you know, you might not have pulled the trigger, but your actions cost Granger his life, so I'm glad I get to take yours." Forge drew his hand back just to watch Francis flinch.

"I'll get you for this. You know that."

Forge turned to Gage, smiling, and then back to Francis. "That's so cliché. I'd have expected something better from a lawyer. But I have something for you. When you're in prison, maybe I'll come visit just to see whose bitch you end up as." He smiled. "Goodbye, Francis. I hope the rest of your life is pure hell." Forge turned and left the office, his legs nearly giving out as soon as he was outside.

"You were amazing," Gage told Forge as he gasped for air. "Maybe you should come into the business with me. You could be the one to extract information, because, damn, I'd hate to be on your bad side." Gage put an arm around him, and Forge leaned into Gage's embrace. This was truly over.

Forge watched as they took Francis away. "Oh, Francis, you're going to need a good lawyer. Don't call here, because this office isn't going to answer." Forge smiled. Hell, he truly grinned for the first time in a week. "Come on. Let's go home."

"And where is that?" Gage asked.

"Wherever you want to take me, as long as it's with you." Forge kissed Gage in front of the FBI and half the law firm. Not that he gave a crap. He'd been through hell and come out the other side with everything he could have ever wanted. Now it was time to rebuild and go on, and the best part was, he knew he didn't have to do it alone.

EPILOGUE

Late December

"WELL, IT'S done," Forge said as he came into the living room. "The law office is closed for good. Everything has been shuttered and the books finalized, attorneys, paralegals and other staff taken care of, and that's a huge monkey off my back." He sat in one of the large black chairs that he loved, putting his feet up on the ottoman. As expected, after the revelations about Francis and who he'd been doing business with, the law practice had imploded on itself. Forge worked with the other attorneys to get them through the fiscal year. He made sure everyone was taken care of and then went through the process of closing the business for good. Not that they were getting any new clients.

The attorneys all drifted away, along with their staff. The hardest part had been subleasing the space, but another firm, started by one of the lawyers who'd worked closely with Granger, had come forward with a plan to start a new practice. Forge arranged for them to take over the lease, and he'd left the furniture and other materials, including the law library, for them. That alone had made the deal sweet for the new firm and got the old firm out of its lease and its one major remaining financial obligation. Even after closing, the firm had had a stellar year, so Forge made sure Granger's parents received part of the payout.

"That's a huge relief," Gage said as he sat on the edge of the ottoman. "What about work?"

"I'm not getting the thrill out of it I was a while ago, so I'm thinking of doing something else. I'm not sure what yet, though. I haven't given notice or anything, but I wanted to talk to you first."

175

"You have a great eye," Gage said, looking around the living room of their large bungalow-style home. Forge had sold his house, and he and Gage had bought something smaller, but with immense amounts of character. "Do what you want to do. You have plenty of money." By the time Forge had settled the estate and found out what Granger had squirreled away, there were millions of dollars that needed to be handled. Forge hired an investment manager, and his nest egg was growing at a rate that outstripped his salary.

"I want to travel and see things. I want us to be able to take trips and go places that are fun. I was thinking Australia in March if you can swing the time away. By then I'll have made a decision." Forge reached over to turn on the Christmas tree that stood in the corner. He loved how festive it made him feel.

"My parents are coming for dinner."

Forge blinked. He had completely forgotten.

"Go ahead and get a shower. I have the gifts wrapped and under the tree for them. They called ten minutes ago to let us know they just crossed the state line." Gage went back in the kitchen. It seemed that both Forge and Gage had discovered a love of cooking. "I have a job that will start after the first of the year."

"What kind of job?" Forge asked as he went down the hall toward their bedroom to undress.

"Interesting one. A singer, famous and all, is going on tour, and they want extra protection, as well as a fresh set of eyes on their security plans, so they called me. I'm going to be spending three weeks on tour with them."

Forge looked up when Gage came in the room. "Who is it?"

"Derrick McCarthy," Gage told him, and Forge nearly fell over. "Yes, the one man on earth that you'd leave me for."

"I don't know about that, but I'd love to have his babies. Wait, that wasn't what I meant." Forge fell onto the bed in a fit of laughter. "See… I get all weird when I think about him."

"Do you want to come with me? I told his people I had a husband who was an interior designer, and apparently Derrick also wants his coach interior redone, and he hates the inside of the house he bought in Saugatuck." Gage stood still, eyebrows raised. It took a few seconds before Forge caught what Gage was trying to tell him.

"Holy crap… I could design for Derrick McCarthy… and he's gay?"

Gage shrugged and left the room.

Forge jumped into the shower, taking a quick one before hopping out, drying himself off, and dressing. He cornered Gage in the kitchen, plastering himself to his back. "He really wants a designer?"

"Yes. And if it works out, it could be a huge door opener. But if you aren't interested in doing that any longer…." Gage was teasing, Forge knew it, and normally he'd have tickled him, but with all the hot stuff around, he just held Gage tighter and kissed his neck. "God, I love you. Tell him I'd be honored to work with him and try to make his home away from home feel more comfortable." Forge didn't move. "And of course I'll be an extra set of eyes for your team." Forge expected an argument, but before Gage could give one, the doorbell rang, and Forge hurried to open the door for his in-laws.

"Merry Christmas," he greeted as Gage's mom and dad walked inside. They came up about once a month, and he and Gage went to see them about as often. They were all working to improve their relationship, and it really seemed to be helping.

Harry greeted him warmly with a handshake, and Shirley hugged him. Gage shared a hug with both his parents, and it spoke a lot about how far they'd come.

"How's business?" Gage asked his dad.

"Better than ever. We reworked a lot of our systems, streamlining things, and now we have more customers and are making more on what we have, so it's a real win." Harry sounded happy as all get-out, and Shirley sported a diamond necklace Forge hadn't seen before, which Shirley kept fingering absently.

"A sparkly present?" Forge asked, and Shirley blushed and beamed at her husband. She then directed Harry to put the gifts under the tree, and they all sat down for a wonderful family evening that lasted well into the night. Forge had prepared the guest room for them, and after they said good night, he and Gage sat in the living room with wine and only the light of the tree.

"In this light you look just like you did when I first met you." Forge leaned in, kissing Gage lightly. "I'll never get over meeting you again… and just when I needed you most." He leaned closer, sliding off the arm of the chair and onto Gage's lap.

"Hey, that goes both ways." Gage drew him closer, exploring his mouth, and the taste of wine and Gage mixed on Forge's lips. "Do you want your present?"

"I already got my present." Forge set his glass on the table beside the chair and drew Gage in for another kiss. He'd gotten the very best present of all, even if it had taken seventeen years and a trip to hell and then back to an amazing life.

DIRK is very much an outside kind of man. He loves travel and seeing new things. Dirk worked in corporate America for way too long and now spends his days writing, gardening, and taking care of the home he shares with his partner of more than two decades. He has a master's degree and all the other accessories that go with a corporate job. But he is most proud of the stories he tells and the life he's built. Dirk lives in Pennsylvania in a century-old home and is blessed with an amazing circle of friends.

Facebook: www.facebook.com/dirkgreyson
Email: dirkgreyson@comcast.net

FLIGHT
OR FIGHT

DIRK GREYSON

Life in the big city wasn't what Mackenzie "Mack" Redford expected, and now he's come home to Hartwick County, South Dakota, to serve as sheriff.

Brantley Calderone is looking for a new life. After leaving New York and buying a ranch, he's settling in and getting used to living at a different pace—until he finds a dead woman on his porch and himself the prime suspect in her murder.

Mack and Brantley quickly realize several things: someone is trying to frame Brantley; he is no longer safe alone on his ranch; and there's a definite attraction developing between them, one that only increases when Mack offers to let Brantley stay in his home. But as their romance escalates, so does the killer. They'll have to stay one step ahead and figure out who wants Brantley dead before it's too late. Only then can they start the life they're both seeking—together.

www.dreamspinnerpress.com

LOST MATE
DIRK GREYSON

Wolf shifter Falco Gladstone knew Carter McCloud was his mate when they were in seventh grade, but school and the foster care system tore them apart. Years later, Falco is second in command of his Michigan pack, serving under an uncle who cares more about his own power than the welfare of their people. The alpha orders Falco to marry and produce offspring—but Falco's already found his mate, and mates are forever.

Carter's lonely life is turned upside down when he detects a familiar scent on the wind. The mates might have found each other, but their happily ever after is far from guaranteed. Falco's commitment to Carter puts him at odds with his uncle's plans, and when one of the alpha's enforcers starts shadowing the couple, something must be done—something that will either cement their relationship or destroy it once and for all.

www.dreamspinnerpress.com

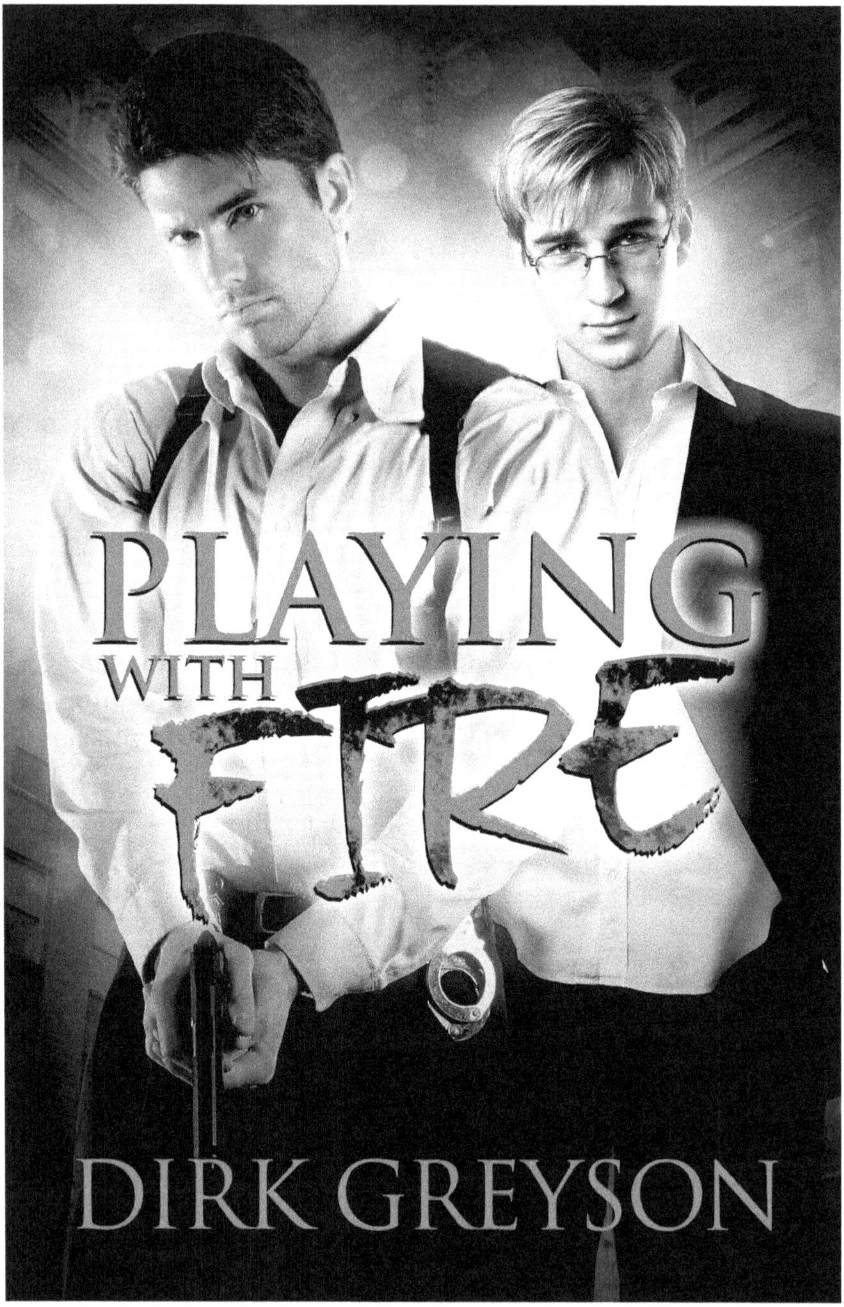
PLAYING
WITH
FIRE
DIRK GREYSON

Jim Crawford was born wealthy, but he turned his back on it to become a police officer. Add that to his being gay, and he's definitely the black sheep of the family.

Dr. Barty Halloran grew up with lessons instead of friends and toys and as a result, became a gifted psychologist… with only an academic understanding of people and emotions.

When Jim's pursuit of a serial killer goes nowhere, he turns to Dr. Halloran for help, and Barty thinks he can get inside the shooter's mind. In many ways, they're two sides of the same coin, which both scares and intrigues him. Together, Jim and Barty make progress on the case—until the stakes shoot higher when the killer turns his attention toward Barty.

To protect Barty, Jim offers to let Barty stay with him, where he discovers the doctor has a heart to go along with his brilliant mind after all. But as they close in on their suspect, the killer becomes desperate, and he'll do anything to elude capture—even threaten those closest to Jim.

www.dreamspinnerpress.com

YELLOWSTONE WOLVES

CHALLENGE the DARKNESS

Dirk Greyson

Yellowstone Wolves: Book One

When alpha shifter Mikael Volokov is called to witness a challenge, he learns the evil and power-hungry Anton Gregor will stop at nothing to attain victory. Knowing he will need alliances to keep his pack together, Mikael requests a congress with the nearby Evergreen pack and meets Denton Arguson, Evergreen alpha, to ask for his help. Fate has a strange twist for both of them, though, and Mikael and Denton soon realize they're destined mates.

Denton resists the pull between them—he has his own pack and his own responsibilities. But Mikael isn't willing to give up. The Mother has promised Mikael his mate, told him he must fight for him, and that only together can they defeat the coming darkness. When Anton casts his sights on Denton's pack, attacks and sabotage follow, pulling Denton and Mikael together to defeat a common enemy. But Anton's threats sow seeds of destruction enough to break any bond, and the mates' determination to challenge the darkness may be their only saving grace.

www.dreamspinnerpress.com

DARKNESS THREATENING

Dirk Greyson

Sequel to *Challenge the Darkness*
Yellowstone Wolves: Book Two

Fredrik is back from college and trying to stay out of his power-hungry brother's way, until his brother takes a prisoner for his pleasure. Unable to tolerate his family's cruelty, Fredrik overcomes his fear to help her escape back to her pack. There, he meets Christopher, and their instant attraction tells him Christopher is the one. However, since the threat of his brother remains, Fredrik is reluctant to pursue a relationship.

Christopher is still figuring out his place in the pack and has been living on his own to avoid making waves with his brother, Mikael. Now he's met his soulmate, and he'll do anything to take care of his love, including rejoining the pack.

With coaxing, Fredrik accepts his feelings, and Christopher's pack gives him the home he's never had. But Fredrick soon realizes he should keep running. His brother is on his tail and will stop at nothing to obtain the power he craves, especially when he realizes the source of the power could be Fredrik himself.

www.dreamspinnerpress.com

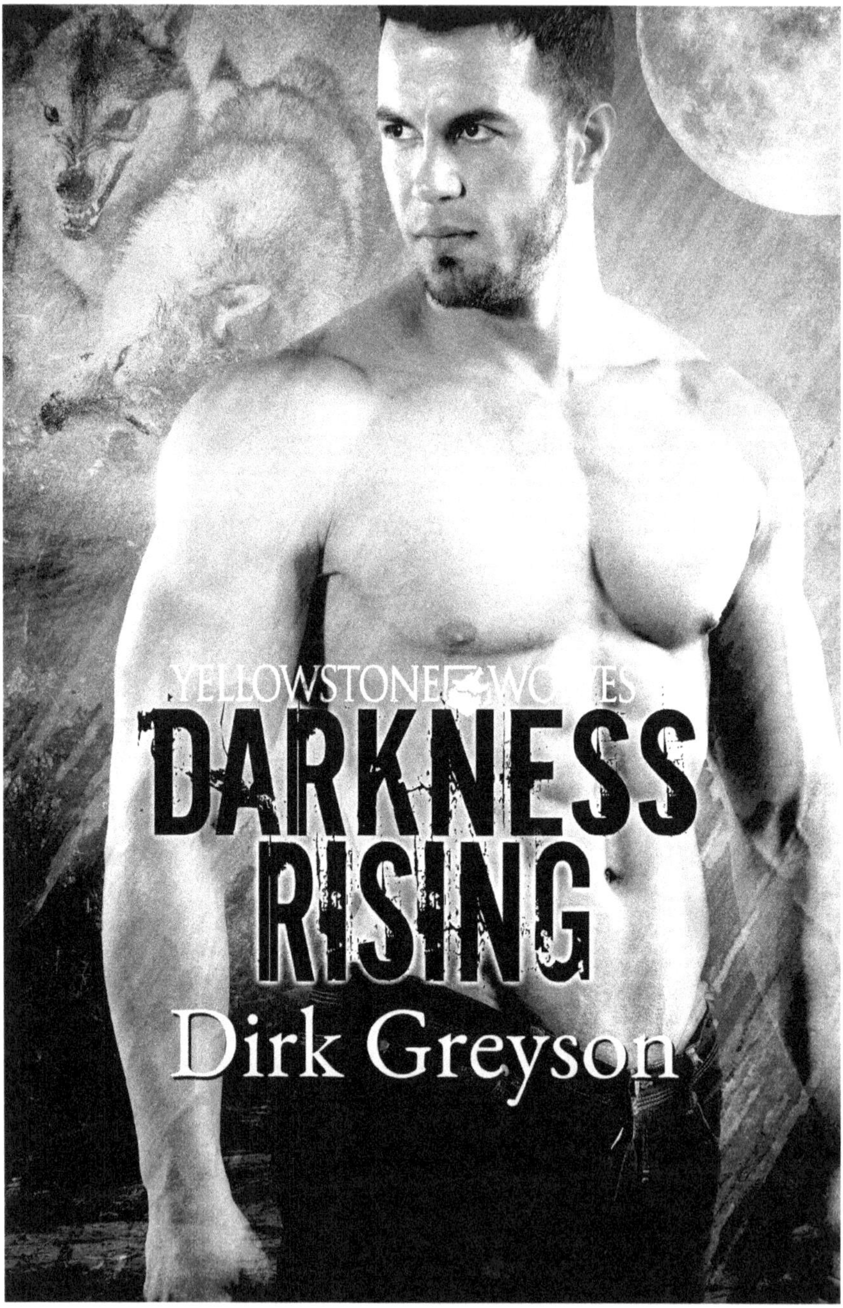
YELLOWSTONE WOLVES
DARKNESS RISING
Dirk Greyson

Sequel to *Darkness Threatening*
Yellowstone Wolves: Book Three

The last thing Tobias, alpha of the small Greenview Pack, expects is to find a lost human asleep in his storage building. As soon as he sets eyes on Pete, Tobias knows they are destined mates. But he cannot act on his attraction, no matter how much he feels compelled. Exposure to the human world could mean the end of their way of life, so he decides to help Pete get a room until he can reunite with the tour group he separated from.

But Tobias's disgraced half brother, Zev, has other ideas. He takes a liking to Pete and decides he wants what Tobias has—both his position as pack leader and his mate. Tobias can't let that happen, but protecting Pete means keeping him close, which only increases the mounting tensions between them.

Duty, protection, desire, and secrecy clash as the darkness within Zev rises to the surface, and only Tobias can save his mate—even if he never plans to tell Pete that's what they are.

www.dreamspinnerpress.com